THE DROWNED WOMAN

THE DROWNED WOMAN

ABIGAIL STEWART

WHiSK(E)Y TIT
NYC & VT

Published in the United States by Whisk(e)y Tit: www.whiskeytit.com. If you wish to use or reproduce all or part of this book for any means, please let the author and publisher know. You're pretty much required to, legally.

ISBN 978-1-952600-13-5

For Brad

PART ONE

"Go west," they told her, as though heeding the call of those primitive ancestors who came before would solve all of her problems. Go west, to the expansive desert, the Sierras, go west until you reach the ocean, where, eventually, you must stop and stare out at eternity for however long you choose.

She held west in her heart and it was enough, for a while. Or, until it wasn't.

Jeanette had her pick of Master's programs, having attained a modest amount of renown when her essay on Louise Bourgeois was published in a collegiate art journal:

"'Eyes represents the totality of the male gaze. Even a woman's own eyes are simply crudely formed breasts, sexual entities, and judged accordingly — both breasts and eyes. In a Surrealist act of dual symbolism, Bourgeois confronts the viewer with literal perception juxtaposed with a woman's sexuality."

Jeanette did not feel particularly passionate about art history, but it was something to do after the end of undergrad. She'd written the entire article in a brief, caffeine-addled haze, unsure if any of it made sense. However, that essay turned out to be the most important thing she'd yet done because it provided a clear path, an escape hatch, a plan. Jeanette decided to sort her options and send herself somewhere warm, somewhere out west.

Sunlight was all she would remember stepping off the plane, it reflected prismatic shapes on the airport terminal's fading, grey walls and she wanted to dip her hands into it, cupping them, filling them with light.

She'd brought only one carry on and a backpack, her earthly possessions mostly consisted of sporadic thoughts and images stored on her laptop, nothing tangible. No one saw her off or welcomed her to her new home. She took a cab to her new university's on-campus housing office and opened an entirely new chapter.

It would strike her later how easy this had been, this starting over, papering over her past life with streaks of sun.

Her new apartment was the first place in which she'd ever lived alone, without parents or roommates. It was one giant square room with a small bathroom and kitchenette attached, funded by her partial scholarship. A room of one's own, Jeanette thought. Immediately, she began to unpack, piles of clothes covered the scuffed, caramel linoleum floor, a cheap facsimile of wood. Without any furniture, the entire place was an open, second floor cavern with views of the parking lot.

The nearby corner store stank of stale, half-smoked cigarettes. A sign advertised, "Keys cut quick!" though one of the lights had burned out and it appeared to just say, "Keys cut..." which was substantially more sinister.

An old, Indian man bent his head crookedly toward the TV which was playing some sort of sports show, he moved only to acknowledge Jeanette's appearance.

She meandered slowly through the aisles filled with tinned meat, bottles of warm soda, cans of beans, candy, chips, and sundry cleaning items. At the end were several shelves of wine. Jeanette observed each of them in turn, running her long fingers across each of the labels decorated with cheap fonts, finally choosing something dry, sparkling, and under ten dollars. She loaded her arms with toilet paper, chips, and precariously balanced the wine between them like a caress.

The man made no effort at conversation, though his mouth moved silently as he tallied up the total bill, sucking his lip in when she proffered a card rather than cash, then begrudgingly providing her with a brown paper bag.

"Thank you," she trilled on her way out. He waved, his back turned already away, facing a screen infinitely more interesting than her.

The empty room echoed with the sounds of passing traffic, the low ceiling lending a claustrophobic feel in the dark. Outside the back window, she could view the kidney-shaped pool, crudely cut into a concrete slab.

It will be warm here all year long, Jeanette reminded herself as she opened the wine.

An absence of kitchenware meant she had to slug the wine straight from the bottle, the foam expanding in her mouth, threatening to overflow. It tickled, she laughed.

Digging around in her carry-on, she found her old black bikini and pulled it on over her sweatpants. She twirled and drank and threw back her head and laughed until the entire room spun with her.

The evening was punctuated by the smell of chlorine, the sound of summer as she jumped gracelessly into the pool, the sun setting behind her.

The advantage of living in a college town was that every semester a fresh influx of students descended on the campus like ants to a sugar trap. In their wake, they left a stream of discarded furniture, clothing, and general flotsam alongside the university's curbs. Eventually, it was moved to a parking lot where it would be disposed of en masse, but in the meantime the curbs were littered with goods.

A thief in the night, Jeanette slunk from her apartment to pillage the spoils.

Her first night out, she prioritized essentials. A toaster, dented aluminum with a crust of crumbs lingering along its lip, an electric tea kettle, a small cardboard box of very mismatched dishes, a mug that read "Maine is for Lovers" and had a lipstick stain along the edge. She went back out for a second load, returning with a surprisingly clean futon mattress, lamp, and low side table.

The second night she dragged back a charmingly threadbare

Oriental style rug and laid it at the foot of her mattress. A couple of fast fashion sundresses were wrapped inside, Jeanette assessed the size and took them as well. Two mahogany bar stools with mustard yellow seats and an antique candelabra that belonged more in a viscount's mansion than a collegiate dorm completed her dining area. Finally, and with much effort, she added a drooping bookshelf which filled up a significant part of her front wall.

Money her scholarship allocated toward books, she spent on a pair of linen pants, wine glasses, and an overstuffed sage green armchair from Goodwill, which she positioned under the lamp for grading and studying. She bought cigarettes, a book of French Impressionist prints, bananas, saltines, and borrowed her textbooks from the library.

On the way back to her apartment one evening, she noticed an overgrown succulent garden, spilling onto the sidewalk — really, being quite a nuisance and getting in everyone's way, if she was being honest. Engaging in her civic duty, Jeanette pruned the plant by moonlight and potted the cuttings in chipped Mason jars she'd found in the apartment complex's dumpster, lining them up along her kitchen windowsill.

Her greatest treasure was something most likely discarded by a young art student: a half finished figure painting, sketchy, on a blue backdrop, with only the face fully defined above a loose, androgynous body. The face was round, cherubic, with hair that fell gently across the forehead in carefully executed, lifelike precision. It made her feel peaceful and was unnecessarily large, an error in judgment probably leading to its unfinished existence. With two thumb tacks substituted for picture hooks, she hung it above her bed.

The box felt cozier now. Jeanette made herbal tea, procured from the corner store, with her new kettle and sat beatifically on the rug.

A stipulation of her scholarship was that she had to TA a class, *Intro to Art History*, in between attending her own lectures and working on a thesis concept she had yet to form fully.

On the first day, Jeanette felt a deep dislike of the students who came to class late, rumpled, reeking of weed and unwashed bodies, of more interesting nights than the ones she had. They were unimpressive specimens.

She dutifully showed slides and went through the lecture notes. They nervously handed her their quizzes, hands shaking a little. The boys' eyes darted from her face to her breasts and back again. She started wearing lower cut shirts to further fluster them.

She graded all the quizzes, sprawled out across her floor, smoking cheap cigarettes. The cigarette smoke often set off the fire alarm, until Jeanette took out its batteries and flushed them down the toilet.

Her own classes were fairly straightforward: *Women in 20th Century Art*, *French Modernism*, *Surrealist Symbolism*. She spent her time thinking and smoking until she had to get out her laptop and sputter forth a paragraph or two, maybe an entire essay. She eloquently and effortlessly discussed the use of color, the meaning of the repetition of a particular bird, "The Milkmaid of Bordeaux."

"Have you thought about a focus for your thesis?" her advising professor asked. He was the teacher of *Intro to Art History*, they were sitting in his office looking at, or pretending to look at, the most recent set of quizzes she'd graded.

The day was particularly warm and Jeanette wore the gauzy yellow sundress she'd found wrapped up in the discarded rug. Her bare feet were adorned with strappy golden sandals and she jiggled one foot, trying not to think about a cigarette.

"Not really," Jeanette admitted.

"Your Bourgeois essay was good, but I think you could push

your examination of female Surrealists further." He said this while staring at her bare legs, her naked knees. Jeanette suspected the reality of his statement was motivated more by his unconscious desire to say 'push' and 'further' together in a sentence directed at her.

"Can I smoke in here?"

The professor stood and obligingly opened a window, his brisk actions were accompanied by a hot gust of air. The professor removed his blazer which had previously concealed the dark sweat stains spreading under his armpits like blood.

Jeanette rose, letting her dress fall to conceal her thighs, one delicate strap fell from her shoulder. Like Sargent's Madame X, she mused, lighting her cigarette, exhaling into the hot breeze. She adjusted the strap back into its appropriate position.

"I suppose there is still quite a bit to say about Bourgeois herself," Jeanette began. "But female Surrealists in general are certainly something to explore. With the advent of Surrealism, women were finally able to assert their desires as creators rather than objects transferred to a creation by a male hand. The Surrealists are rife with sexual power."

Jeanette turned back to the professor, he was definitely devouring her with his eyes.

"And so many were egregiously overlooked during their lifetimes, only known now through grand retrospectives. Yes, I agree it could be an interesting topic," she drawled, making pointed eye contact with him.

The professor blinked awareness back into his face, then slapped the desk with the same decisive motion he'd used to open the window, employing his entire body.

"Well, it's decided then! These quizzes all look good, Jeanette."

Jeanette accepted her dismissal and stubbed the cigarette out on the window sill. Her sandals slapped softly underfoot as she retreated down the hallway embraced by an aura of lingering smoke.

The seasons never seemed to change and Jeanette found herself easily adjusting to her new reality. She didn't need an extra set of clothes and happily lived in her sundresses and breezy pants.

When winter break arrived, it was still 70 degrees.

Jeanette had passed her courses and submitted her official thesis proposal, she'd graded final exams alongside a pack of cigarettes and airplane bottles of Scotch she'd found for 99 cents at the corner store. The small amount kept her honest. Soon, the exams blurred together into a hazy mess and she began arbitrarily assigning grades based on her prior knowledge of the student, accompanying each blazing A, B, C with a blithe comment, "Nice work!" "Interesting point!" "Could use more elaboration here."

It was over now and she had nowhere to go, no commitments. The evening sun lit her small box, lending it a warm glow that felt comforting.

Jeanette lay across her armchair, legs dangling off one side, a book lay discarded on her abdomen. She blew smoke rings at the ceiling. She was aware of how she should have felt, accomplished, pleased with herself, but mostly she felt bored. She felt her ankle twitch impatiently.

Boredom was a familiar feeling.

She pictured the empty, blue skies of her youth, the winters of bleak, endless snowstorms, nothing but white without variation for months. Snowed in. The damp smell of rain boots, woolen coats, and their basement permeated each memory. There was always a hushed atmosphere, as though sound had also been dampened with the silence of snow. Sometimes she wouldn't speak for days. Not that anyone noticed.

Jeanette left for college, art, an entire world of color. Though she'd first majored in psychology, then studio art, before landing in her current degree at the second college she attended. Every iteration eventually reached a tipping point. Art history had opened a new door for her.

The sun sank lower and Jeanette raised her body slightly to turn on the lamp.

Men were just as transient. Her only permanent memory was the red rose tattoo on her hip. Inhaling her cigarette, Jeanette leaned her head back against the armchair and felt the exquisite pain of the needle on her virginal skin. It had brought her to the brink of orgasm. She'd been too afraid to replicate the experience, afraid it would become a quick fix to her feeling of being stuck. The external pain allowed her to go outside her psyche and experience something in the present moment, it was then she felt most tethered to the earth.

The tattoo remained, the artist she broke up with a week later.

As Jeanette sank deeper into a reverie and considered how many airplane bottles of Scotch remained, a group of companions, laughing loudly, passed along the walking path that lined their parking lot. Their jovial voices crowded into her apartment, slinking under the door and enticing her.

Her ankle twitched twice more and Jeanette jerked herself upward.

She smudged a bit of lipstick on her lips and, after a brief inspection, applied dry shampoo to her hair. The dress, which had fit her perfectly earlier in the semester, now hung a bit around her hips. Overall, she felt the appearance was acceptable enough for the local dive bar.

Her pocketbook didn't contain anything more than her personal and student IDs, apartment keys, and a single twenty dollar bill.

She joined the small contingent of people walking toward the strip of student bars ahead. The joking friends had long since passed, but the night had a hint of something magical. Perhaps it was the end of the semester or the changing of the seasons or the uncharacteristic warmth, but Jeanette felt her decision to leave the apartment had been the right one.

She passed other apartment buildings and small houses as she walked. Each window presented a tableau of hidden life: families, couples, a TV flashing garish blue into the night with no one to watch it except passing phantoms. Living on the second floor, Jeanette rarely wondered what her own life might reflect to those who passed by, she just closed the blinds.

The first bar was a blatant undergrad attraction with shuffleboard and bocce ball and a plethora of outdoor picnic tables that allowed students to feel they were somewhere else, camping perhaps, rather than in a markedly bland suburban.

Jeanette walked on, to the bar she felt most comfortable, its unwelcome wood and metal facade was windowless and vaguely threatening. She slid into the darkness like an octopus returning to its hidden home under the guise of ink. Men old enough to be her father played pool in the back, tables were occupied with professors in deep, philosophical conversation and townies who were playing quarters. Every once in a while a large shout would erupt from one or the other for entirely different reasons, either a quarter had landed squarely in the shot glass or someone mentioned Marxism.

She slid onto one of the red leather barstools, the plush top was soft, torn, sunken slightly, well-loved by the unloved.

A grizzled woman in a black tank top with a tattooed armband of thorns that read "RIP Missy" asked what she'd like.

"A Scotch, please. Neat."

"Well or you want something fancy?"

"Well is fine."

Jeanette knew well liquor was only $5 and she had a budget after all.

The woman sloshed a definite overpour of Scotch into a smudged glass and Jeanette took a sip, smiled her approval. The woman grimaced in return and walked away. She had a long white braid that hung limply just above her buttocks. Jeanette was more intrigued by the tattoos peaking out from behind it.

She shivered a little, pleasurable, and took another warming sip of Scotch.

By the end of her first drink, she felt her ears pinking a little and someone else's eyes on her. Down the bar a good looking older man caught her eye. She smiled instinctively, on cue, the way Midwesterners do when someone looks their way. She had a big open smile, not a coy grin. It didn't take much, he was one stool away from her in less than a moment.

"What are you having?" he asked.

"Scotch."

"Two more?" the man asked their bartender who grimaced again in response.

Jeanette felt the desire to apologize to her, to explain she didn't actually know this man. Instead, she accepted the offer of a drink.

"So, where are you from? I don't think I've seen you here before."

"Oh, it's my first visit," she lied.

"You live nearby?"

"Not really," the second lie was easier.

Their Scotches appeared, again on cue.

"Cheers," he offered.

"To what?" she asked.

"To you!"

She smiled, coyly this time, and took a sip of her drink.

Jeanette sold him small jigsaw pieces of her life: she was a graduate student in a humanities field, she hadn't lived here long, she liked plants. It wasn't enough for him to complete the puzzle, but enough to get another Scotch.

After the third, she felt woozy, though not drunk. Her tolerance had been fortified by the late nights of grading and accompanying airplane bottles, but when she thought back to the entirety of her day, Jeanette realized she hadn't eaten anything since peanut butter on toast that morning.

She was still calculating her caloric intake when she realized the man, Peter, was speaking to her. He had a few days' worth of stubble on his chin, it was dark, peppered with grey. His fingernails were trimmed and clean, she liked that.

"I'm sorry, what was that?" she asked.

"I said, do you want to get out of here?"

Jeanette weighed her options for a blink, before answering, "Sure, sounds good."

He paid their tab and led her out to his car.

"It's a rental," he apologized.

"It's nice," she offered.

He smiled at her, put his hand on her thigh as they drove the short distance in the darkness together. He was staying in a hotel, one of the nicer ones near the university.

"I'm here doing some consultation work for the college," he explained.

She nodded, unsure if he'd already told her that or not.

Once they were inside the room, he offered to fix them some minibar drinks and Jeanette wasn't sure what to do with her hands. She leaned awkwardly against the wall, he handed her gin in a plastic cup intended for use with the hotel provided mouthwash.

One sip in and he was on her, kissing her with far too much tongue. Jeanette moved her own tongue out of the way to accommodate his. She let him slip off her panties, lift the dress up over her head, she hadn't been wearing a bra, which seemed to further turn him on. He laid her across the bed and flicked his tongue over the rose tattoo.

"Hot," he whispered, before moving to her breasts.

He was undressed just as quickly, though she didn't watch. They kissed again, but Jeanette could tell he was straining to get on with it.

It took him a moment to get the condom on and she halfheartedly pumped at his penis while she waited. Once he accomplished the most difficult task of the evening, she straddled him and stared up at the ceiling until he'd finished, her inclined neck a facsimile of enjoyment, desire.

"That was amazing," he whispered into her hair before passing out in a booze induced coma.

Once she was certain he'd fallen asleep, Jeanette turned the TV to a comedy show that replayed itself in endless syndication and ate all of the peanuts in the minibar.

The next morning, Jeanette woke abruptly, not knowing where she was. Everything was hotel white and smelled far too clean. She also wasn't used to being fully elevated off the ground, her futon mattress only lay six inches or so off the floor. The plush hotel bed felt much like a pitcher plant's trap, a little too convenient.

Peter emerged from the bathroom adjusting his tie, Jeanette instinctively pulled the comforter up to her neck.

"Good, you're awake."

"Yes, sorry I overslept," she began to edge off the bed in an attempt to take her leave gracefully.

"Don't worry about it. I have meetings until the evening, take your time getting ready." He bent over to kiss her forehead, an act that struck Jeanette as fatherly. "Thanks for last night, I had fun." He grabbed his blazer off the hanger by the door and, with a quick smile, evaporated into the hallway.

Jeanette waited for his footsteps to hush in the hallway, then she immediately called room service and turned the TV back on.

It felt like such a luxury, television. She didn't own one in her small apartment and her primary entertainment was the shouting of her neighbors, cigarettes, and her art textbooks. In something of a stupor, she watched the end of one show and started another when someone knocked at the door.

Jeanette rose with languid ease, already at home with hotel life, tying the white terrycloth robe that hung on the bathroom door loosely at her waist.

The server produced a plate of warm toast, scrambled eggs, a side of bacon, extra crispy like she'd asked. There was also a large carafe of coffee with sugar and cream. Jeanette ushered him in and he placed the platter at the foot of her bed, she gave him a five, leftover from the twenty dollar bill she'd brought with her last night.

Alone again, she slathered the toast with pat after pat of butter, layered each time with an individual packet of strawberry jam. She devoured the eggs and bacon and poured herself another cup of coffee from the carafe. Crumbs of toast lingered on her breasts and she wiped her greasy hands on the robe leaving lurid streaks of yellow brown.

Wolfish hunger in all its forms raised a head every few days, Jeanette was used to her own feral instincts.

Once sated, she lay back against the pillows and burped heartily.

In the dress from the night before, Jeanette decided to stroll through campus. Her apartment was just on the opposite side and it was a nice day.

She hadn't given Peter her number or another thought since leaving the hotel room. With no hunger to distract her, everything seemed crystalline, beautiful.

How could I have ever been bored here? Jeanette wondered.

The trees were just starting to change colors, despite it being December, and the gold and crimson leaves fell delicately to the ground where they were inevitably crushed underfoot, creating a red carpet of foliage upon which Jeanette now trod.

Life seemed possible again, she decided.

Campus was quiet, only a few students running to and fro from the mostly shut down cafeteria to their winter mini-mester classes.

Outside the Psychology building, an older grad student, or younger professor, sat smoking on the concrete wall that ran the perimeter of the building's facade. He looked boyish and a little forlorn. Jeanette, buoyed by the weather and her fresh perspective, approached him.

"Can I bum one?" she asked, indicating the pack of American Spirits he had atop his knee.

He nodded, passed the pack toward her.

"Light?"

He leaned in with a silver lighter, monogrammed with something she noticed, and obliged her request. His eyes were a very particular color of green. Pine needles, she decided.

Jeanette exhaled happily.

"You have a class?" he asked, his voice had a trace of European accent.

"No, just passing through. I'm on break."

"You didn't go home?"

She shrugged, not inclined to divulge much.

He seemed satisfied not to pursue it any further and they smoked companionably looking out at the campus lawn strewn with leaves, squirrels darting in and out of piles.

She stubbed her cigarette out on the concrete barrier, shoved the butt in the unattractive plastic bins they placed all over campus to deter students from leaving cigarettes in flowerbeds.

"Thanks," she offered.

"See you around," he flashed a quick grin before returning to his inspection of the leaf piles.

Jeanette left him there.

Back at her apartment, she showered. The hot water washed away some of the lingering film of the previous evening. The heat from the shower always added a layer of humidity to the entirety of her small apartment. During the summer, it was impossible to disperse, but today she opened a window, then proceeded to drink glass after glass of water from the tap while wrapped in a ratty, faded red towel that had followed her around since undergrad. The cool air raised goosebumps on her arms.

Winter break waned and Jeanette spent her days alternating between cups of herbal tea with black instant coffee, the two cheapest things in the corner store. The old Indian man knew her now, his name was Vihaan and they said hello to one another. He didn't bat an eye when she came in for Scotch and cigarettes or orange juice and crackers.

One night, when it was raining, Jeanette lingered and they watched most of a Bollywood movie together in silence. She sat on a metal stool opposite the cash register and he passed her a paper cup of milky chai tea from a thermos. When the rain stopped, she thanked him and left, he nodded and never mentioned it again. When she thought about it, Jeanette imagined he was the closest thing she currently had to a friend.

Another night, Jeanette found an abandoned box of books near her apartment dumpster. She did a quick sort and rescued an armful from their cardboard prison. Most of them were English 101 classics that she had pretended to read in undergrad, skimming or enlisting CliffsNotes instead.

She spent the rest of her break reading *Madame Bovary*, *Pride and Prejudice*, *The Count of Monte Cristo*. When she'd finished reading each one, she added it to her bookshelf. The shelf held its new charges proudly and, with an additional smattering of art books, it was beginning to look quite studious in here, Jeanette decided.

She didn't go back to the dive bar.

The new semester brought a hum of renewed energy. Jeanette didn't have to teach classes that semester, instead she took an extra independent study course and began to research her thesis.

She'd mostly avoided her mentor professor since that day in his office, when the weather was still warm. He hadn't said anything to her and allowed her to leave her written drafts in his office mailbox which he then returned to her student mailbox, with edits.

Jeanette felt this was the best case scenario and savored her freedom.

She spent hours in the student library occasionally researching, but mostly because it was warm. Right as it had gotten cold in earnest, Jeanette had discovered the heating in her apartment did not work and, according to her neighbors, had not worked for some time.

She watched busy undergrads study for exams, flirt with one another in the reading carousels, and spend more time surfing the web than doing any meaningful research. Jeanette counted herself among them and used the computer stalls to skim articles from which she'd extract one meaningful quote or idea, then congratulate herself on a job well done before returning to one of the orphaned classic novels, at that time *Moby Dick*. It was her own version of a roundabout education.

One of her courses this semester was a late start, meaning she had a couple of weeks before needing to attend lectures. It was called Religion in Modern Art and sounded vague enough to stir her interest as well as allow her some latitude in composing equally vague essay responses.

When the day came to begin classes, she strolled in a little late to find the green eyed man with whom she'd shared a smoke behind the podium.

"Professor Vaughn will teach the class, I am merely his grading arm," the man finished. "My name is Oliver, please email me with any immediate requests or concerns and I will forward them to Professor Vaughn. Make sure you take a syllabus and I will see you on Thursday."

Everyone moved to leave. Sheepishly, having just sat down, Jeanette rose to grab one of the syllabi fanned across the desk.

"Hello," he was looking at her.

"Hi, sorry I was late."

"That's alright. In fact, it seems appropriate for a late start class, yes?"

She smiled.

"Would you like to smoke with me?"

Out of cigarettes for a few days now, or until her student loan came through, Jeanette nodded a little too eagerly. They retreated together to the tree where it was deemed an appropriate distance away from the corridor of polite society to engage in their officious habit.

"Are you an art major then?" Jeanette asked.

"No, psychology actually. I offered to TA for Professor Vaughn this semester because I've taken the class and, to be honest, I needed the money."

He lit her cigarette. She considered again how he had a European gentlemanliness as he leaned in close to her. He smelled like cloves and tobacco.

"I TAed last semester, for Professor Singh. But I have more scholarship money this semester and decided to do an independent study instead," she explained.

"Makes sense. What is your focus?"

"Female Surrealists."

"Particularly?"

"Louise Bourgeois."

Oliver nodded and made an approving noise in his throat.

"Well, best of luck with Ms. Bourgeois. I, unfortunately, must go and report to my master the goings on of today's first class."

"Don't tell him I was late."

Oliver chuckled, a soft sound like pebbles falling in water. Jeanette was taken aback by how much she wanted to hear it again.

"It was the first thing I was going to say, but now I've reconsidered."

They smiled at each other, he left her holding the depleted end of her cigarette under the scarlet overhang. Only then did

Jeanette realize she felt rather cold.

◇

The semester passed as semesters do, both slow and fast at the same time. Each day seemed a tedious stringing together of moments, then inevitable surprise when a week had passed and assignments previously put off were soon due. Jeanette's own verbose essays were composed by candlelight at the bar in her apartment.

"Frida Kahlo's Self Portrait, 1953 illustrates the places on her body that she felt were not her own, the places that were injured, painful, and necessitated 'fixin.' Although her body was a living wound, she was able to display herself in a way that branded her as an art object, a curiosity, and decidedly feminine, rather than a cripple. In this way, her brand endures, emblazoned on tote bags with a flower crown, a model to the modern feminine ideal."

Jeanette read The Diary of Frida Kahlo and marveled at the depiction of the self through visual medium, at Frida's life of pain and perseverance. She wondered how she might fashion her own self-portrait. Collage, mixed media, would be her medium: a mismatched patchwork of ash, tattered book pages, and lipstick kissed off before a night out.

Not for the first time, Jeanette wished she were an artist rather than an art historian. She was certain her inability to create something new spoke to a deficit within herself. And so, instead, she wrote responses to the slides they were shown in class, staving off the impending existential crisis that burdens all artistic souls.

She didn't see Oliver again until midterms, when he reappeared for review day. She took notes dutifully and avoided making eye contact. He wasn't her type and she didn't want him getting any ideas. However, when her midterm was returned, marked in a few places with the same sort of notations she'd employed in the previous semester, her heart warmed toward him slightly. She imagined the ballpoint of his red pen sliding smoothly across her essay, engaging with her words. She shivered.

The weather warmed again and it was as though springtime had never left. Everyone ran outside in sandals and shorts, they called to one another across the grassy fields, and Jeanette walked among them.

She sold some textbooks to the used bookstore on campus. As she was pocketing the forty dollars, she bumped right into Oliver.

"Oh, hi," she shouted. "Sorry, you scared me."

"I spotted you looking over your earnings."

"Not much of one, but I might have enough for a beer."

Mentally she calculated that she needed enough for toothpaste, toilet paper, and her electricity bill as well.

"I was just about to head to the pub, would you like to join?"

She shrugged, "Sure."

The pub in reference was less than a block from the university. They carded everyone and the bartenders were either mean or high. At this time of day, high was more likely. The bar itself was all dark wood, built in booths with worn mosaic countertops. The bar had a polyurethane coat over it that sealed in old collegiate newspapers, baseball cards, international currency, small plastic toys, and matchbooks from all over the United States. Jeanette stared into the flotsam, mesmerized.

"It's like looking into someone else's soul," she said.

"Quite a time capsule," Oliver added.

He ordered them two pilsners and they settled in at a table in the back, one where the booth hugged a corner and you had no choice but to sit caddy-corner to one another, leaning forward on your elbows, hopeful someone might say something interesting.

Jeanette didn't have much love for beer, but sipped the foamy mug slowly, her hands wrapped around the cool glass, leaving behind a memory of her fingerprints. She wished it were Scotch. Then, she realized Oliver was speaking to her.

"You weren't listening, were you?" he smirked.

"No, sorry. I was thinking."

"It's fine, I was just asking if you'd been to the beach here?"

"I don't have a car, but I hear it's nice."

He looked visibly taken aback. "How do you not have a car?"

"I just don't. I don't go anywhere except campus and home."

"Well, you've officially made me depressed Ms. Jeanette. I had no idea you were such a study-bug."

She didn't know how to respond, so she just took another sip of beer.

"So, what do you do for fun then?"

"I read, mostly."

She didn't add, sometimes pick up guys at bars or watch Bollywood movies with my close friend who owns the corner store nearest my apartment.

"Anything interesting lately?"

"I've been re-reading some of the classics I missed out on in undergrad."

"Admirable. Most people I know miss them, then dismiss them entirely without much of a backward glance."

"I came upon a box of them, I'm still working my way through Jane Austen and *Moby Dick* right now."

"You're a conquerer!" Oliver raised his glass and clinked it against hers. "Like I told you, my graduate degree will be in psychology, my undergrad though, that was literature. So, I respect your undertaking."

"Many thanks," Jeanette faked a little bow. "So, why psychology?"

"The mind is a fascinating thing. I also thought it might make me a better writer, to understand humans on a deeper level."

A waitress stopped by the table then, she was clad in short black shorts, her half apron covered them entirely, and a tank top. "Can I get y'all anything?"

"A Scotch and an ashtray," Jeanette said quickly.

"Make that two," Oliver added.

"Two ashtrays?"

"Sure."

Jeanette watched his eyes and silently credited him with not openly checking out her ass as she walked away.

"You write then?" she asked.

"Sorry?"

"You said you're majoring in psychology because you want an insight into people for writing. What do you write?"

"This and that. Short stories mostly. I haven't touched upon my big idea yet."

The waitress returned with two Scotches and two ashtrays. They both took out cigarettes and chased the action with a sip of Scotch before inhaling. It was so in sync that Jeanette felt an invisible forcefield had corralled them together at that table and they were all alone.

"Anyway," Oliver continued, "my friends and I want to start up a literary magazine. We've been talking about it for a while, but everyone is doing them online these days. There's no barrier to entry, but maybe that's a good thing, more equitable and in line with the current state of things. I just think there's potential there. The hardest thing would probably be finding interested writers. There are so many wannabes on a college campus, it's hard to discern who isn't just full of bullshit."

"And, in the meantime, you can publish your friends," Jeanette joked.

Oliver glowered, exhaled his cigarette down toward the floor.

"Have you got a name for it?" She tried to press on, gloss over.

"*Parenthesis Press*, or *Elliptical*."

Jeanette nodded slowly, intending to indicate she thought they were scholarly choices, though she personally found alliteration somewhat trite.

"We are aiming to launch it by next semester, hopefully we can ask some students to submit and get a real movement going. You should submit something."

"Oh yeah?"

"Sure, I read your work all the time, remember? I'm basically already your editor."

Jeanette thought again of his pen running in tandem alongside her words.

"Good point," she raised her glass of Scotch in a mock salute.

"How'd you end up here?" Oliver asked suddenly. "You just don't seem the normal type," he blushed, "I mean that in a good way."

Jeanette watched the way his blush creeped across his nose to his cheeks, highlighting his freckles.

"Oh, I threw a dart at a map," she replied.

"Really?"

"Sure. What about you?"

"My parents moved to America when I was in elementary school, but they still insisted I take French lessons, so I never really acquired the requisite American accent. As I'm sure you've noticed."

She shrugged noncommittally.

"Right, well, it usually comes up sooner as a talking point."

"Well, I'm not particularly nosy."

"I like that about you."

"Do you want another?"

"Sure."

She flagged down the waitress and they spent the next quarter of an hour discussing the differences between French fries and pommes frites.

Finally the sun began to set and the younger collegiate set rolled in, crowding the bar with their fake IDs and obviously hesitant drink choices. Jeanette knew from her younger days that you had to have a drink in mind before you approached the bar, you shouldn't ask for recommendations, you go up and confidently order a cranberry and vodka like you've been doing it all your life.

She explained all of this to Oliver who listened intently.

"You sound like you know what you're talking about."

"I did, once upon a time."

He let her split the tab when she insisted, using most of the forty dollars she'd procured earlier that afternoon. They exited the bar together into a sunwarmed evening.

"Well, this was nice. An unexpected addition to a boring afternoon," Oliver said, their eyes adjusting to the outdoor light, the absence of smoke.

"It was. Maybe we can repeat it sometime."

"I'd like that."

Then, in a quick gesture, he brought her right hand to his mouth and kissed her knuckles gently, his lips barely making contact with her skin. It reminded Jeanette of when he'd lit her cigarette before, some holdover of genteel manners from his upbringing, she imagined.

"Good night, Jeanette," he added, before turning on his heel and stalking back to campus, the sleeves of his sweater pulled up haphazardly around his elbows.

"Good night," she said, a little more quietly, before returning alone to her apartment.

She stopped in to see Vihaan, he was watching a soccer match on the TV behind the counter. He didn't move when she entered. Jeanette walked the rows of the small store, latching upon a package of chocolate chip cookies, then a few single bananas because they made her feel healthier and the Scotch was sloshing heavily in her stomach now.

"Hi Vihaan," she offered, once at the counter.

"Oh, it's you."

"Yes, I'm back."

He rang up her goods, nodding as he did so. Jeanette pretended he was approving of her purchases. She gathered her items in her arms, she'd stopped asking for a bag now, and readied herself to leave.

"Wait a moment," Vihaan stopped her.

He disappeared under the counter, then popped back up with a small white paper bag.

"Here," he shoved it at her. Grease had soaked through one side, creating a transparent window.

"What is it?"

"Samosas, my sister is in town. She makes too much food."

Jeanette felt her eyes fill with overemotional Scotch tears, "Thank you."

He waved her off and turned back to the soccer match, Jeanette took that moment to escape with the remnants of her dignity.

She ate the two samosas over the sink. They were filled with peas and potatoes and the flaky crust still held a memory of warmth, it melted in her mouth. She moaned with repressed pleasure like an animal in heat.

Jeanette met Oliver a few more times, always at the same bar, and each time they lingered a little longer, spoke a little more frankly with each other. Their evenings together staved off Jeanette's dangerous flights of fancy and she was able to robotically go about her days.

One evening, a week or so before their final exams, Jeanette invited him back to her apartment.

There had been little to no physical contact between them aside from a chaste kiss on the cheek, but tonight, the plants in her apartment were looking especially cheery and she felt like sharing their lushness, as well as her airplane bottle stash.

Oliver walked slightly behind her as they meandered from the bar to the street that led to her apartment.

"You live over here?" he asked, observing the area.

"Yes."

"Isn't it a little, well, sketchy?"

"Not really. There haven't been any break-ins or shootings, at least not that I'm aware of, it's too close to campus."

His eyes widened slightly.

Jeanette paused and took a moment to view it from his

perspective. Sure, there were some overflowing bags of trash and graffiti tagged corridors, but she was certain no crimes beyond the occasional drug deal were happening in this area. And she didn't do drugs, so it hardly affected her.

She continued walking.

They reached her apartment which, from the outside, had the appearance of an old roadside motel. The concrete steps that led to her floor were lined with an iron railing that had peeled back in places to reveal several layers of different colored paint. For the first time since moving in, she felt self-conscious of its facade. Normally, she enjoyed the vintage vibe.

Jeanette pushed the door open and turned on her lamp, she headed directly for the kitchen.

Oliver remained in the doorway.

"You have an interesting style," he commented.

"Isn't this stuff great? I got it all for free, or really cheap. It's shocking what some people throw away."

"You don't say," he quipped.

She ignored him and poured herself a drink. "You want one?"

He stepped in further to view her offering and cocked his eyebrow up.

"Sure."

She handed him a glass, stained blue around the rim, one of her free finds. She placed the small bottle inside of it, suddenly disinclined to pour it for him, and pushed it across the formica bar that currently separated them.

Oliver took the hint and poured his own drink, then took the glass with him to inspect the contents of her bookshelf.

"Oh, you have *Naked Lunch*. What did you think?"

"I didn't finish it."

He looked disappointed.

"I'm reading *Sense and Sensibility* right now."

He didn't respond.

"My neighbor gave me this record player when he was moving out, well, when he was going to serve some lapsed jail time. Same thing." Jeanette moved toward the bookshelf where an all-in-one record player sat. "He only had a few jazz records, but I like to listen to them before I go to bed." She picked up Miles Davis's *Kind of Blue* and put it on, the rhythmic sound of trumpet and snare filled her small apartment.

Jeanette could easily read Oliver's face, she'd seen it before on people she'd met, friends she'd brought home in her youth. They always had that same slightly disbelieving expression, as thought they'd imagined an entirely different life for her and were disappointed by, or maybe just uncomfortable with, being forced to re-imagine her in a new setting. It was the same way a viewer of art might see a painting one way, then read the artist's title and realize they had it entirely upside down. It affects one's perception.

"Anyway, I've got an early class tomorrow. I should probably spend some time studying," Jeanette commented, still looking at the record player.

"Oh," Oliver replied.

"Yeah."

He replaced the now empty cup on the bar and walked to the door. There was no kiss on the cheek or knuckles and Jeanette closed the door behind him without further conversation. She turned up Miles Davis, finished her drink, and swiveled her hips back to the kitchen to get another. The evening sunlight pushed geometric shapes across her floor and she dipped her toes in each sunbeam. She also resolved to only invite people to her apartment from now on, if simply to see their reactions, a peeling back to their base forms.

During their Religion in Modern Art final exam review, still resolutely ignoring him, Jeanette received her practice exam back with a note attached. She recognized the looping writing in red pen and immediately scowled.

J, Come to the beach with me after final , I will make it up to you. – O

She felt Oliver's eyes on her from the podium and considered, albeit briefly, crumpling the note and dropping it on the floor. On the other hand, she did really want to see the beach. Shoulders back, face impassive, she approached him.

"Fine," she said.

His face lifted, "I'll pick you up on Saturday."

"I'm not inviting you in."

She turned and walked away, a secret smile spreading inside of her like warm butter.

Oliver was outside her apartment building at 9AM sharp the following Saturday morning. As promised, Jeanette did not invite him in but descended the stairs regally with a small tote carrying beach essentials: a change of clothes, towel, book, sunscreen. She wore her only swimsuit, the black bikini she'd christened her apartment in, under a sundress, and topped her head with a pair of comically large black cat-eyed sunglasses she'd found at a gas station.

"Fancy," Oliver said as she climbed in.

"Yes, I'm very 'Elizabeth Taylor goes slumming,'" she agreed.

"If only I could put the top down."

"So where are we going?"

"My friends have this house on the beach and I thought we could meet them there."

"Okay," Jeanette agreed.

Oliver turned on the radio and a wailing female voice filled the space between them. Jeanette chose not to bring up her hurt feelings, instead she let the woman's voice be the communique of forgiveness.

They drove up a winding coastal highway lined with evergreens on one side, an open expanse of blue ocean on the other. It seemed impossible for the two to coexist, more impossible still for their passage to be the dividing line between the two worlds. Jeanette rolled down the window and smelled the salt air.

Each bend gave way to a small coastal town, the houses seemed to incrementally increase in size as they traveled down the coast. Eventually, Oliver turned in at one of the beachside monoliths.

"This is it?" Jeanette asked, hiding her hesitancy with a steady voice.

He nodded.

The facade was white stucco, there were two stories encased in windows overlooking the waves, and a few other cars already in the driveway. It looked intentionally unobtrusive, as though the owner wanted it to blend into the sand, hiding any material wealth.

As they approached the door, Jeanette could hear the jovial banter of distant people on the back deck, a party in progress to which she was technically uninvited. Peering through the front window, she could see all the way through the house and onwards still toward the beach. She paused, anticipating that they might knock, but Oliver simply opened the door and charged inside. Jeanette had no choice but to follow his lead.

The house was grandly appointed with minimalist, neutral decor that leant all focus to the natural art outside the wall of windows. Above the fireplace was a sculpture Jeanette recognized as a Rodin replica. The stark darkness of the metal sucked all of the light toward it and she had to applaud the placement.

Oliver, meanwhile, was shaking hands with an older, barrel chested man clad in a preppy shorts and deck shoe combination that belied his age.

"Uncle Bertie, so good to see you," Oliver laughed.

"Oliver, it's been too long," he sloshed his glass of white wine dangerously close to a mohair chaise lounge.

"This is Jeanette."

Her cue. She stepped forward and proffered her hand.

"It's been a while since Oliver brought a girl to one of these," the man laughed, then shook her up and down vigorously, as though he were working an old-fashioned water pump. "Have fun, kids," he called before wandering back outside.

Jeanette leaned over to Oliver and growled into his neck, "Did you call him 'uncle'?"

"Yes, I didn't want to alarm you, but this is a little family get together."

In all the iterations of who Jeanette had considered she might encounter that afternoon, Oliver's family had not even made the list.

"Why didn't you tell me? I would have dressed nicer," she protested, knowing she probably wouldn't have.

"You look great," he whispered in her ear.

She glowered at him until an impeccably dressed woman approached them. Her hair was neatly coiffed into a careful brown bob, her skin gleamed with the aura of time for sleep and money for skin products. She wore a tailored navy blue sheath dress and had bare feet with classic red toenails. Obviously a weak attempt at bohemia, Jeanette thought.

"Ollie." She greeted him with two kisses on each cheek.

"Mum. This is Jeanette."

Of course she was Oliver's mother, everything made perfect sense. Her eyes took in Jeanette's windswept, sun-streaked hair, her cheap dress with visible bikini straps, and pursed her lips into a lemony smile.

"Charmed. You can call me Adele." Then, turning back to her son, "You didn't call to tell us you were bringing a friend. But never fear, Bertie picked up far too much wine and lobster tail as usual, plenty for everyone."

Her voice had the same French lilt as Oliver's, except less relaxed. Everything she said felt clipped.

"Well, let's go outside." Adele ushered them out like school children.

A group of fifteen or so people mingled on the deck which gracefully dove into the white sand where a couple of children were playing.

"Everyone! Ollie is here! And he brought... what was your name again, darling?"

"Jeanette."

"Jenay!"

The congregation looked up briefly, then returned to their conversations. A group of younger people approached them.

"My cousins," Oliver whispered.

"Ollie!" The pack descended on him with much hugging and jostling of the shoulders.

"So, what's your actual name?" a dark-haired female cousin asked, leaning closer to Jeanette.

"Jeanette."

"Aunt Adele gets everyone's names wrong," his male cousin chortled.

"She called me Myrtle for years, of course, it was mostly because she hates my mum. Anyway, I'm Marian, that's Thomas."

Jeanette nodded and plastered a smile to her face as they began to chat.

"You need wine," Marian interjected, "Ollie, fetch her some wine!"

"Better do what Marian says, she's been a real bitch this week," Thomas joked.

"I'm on my period, asshole," Marian shoved him. "My brother, a real charmer. Anyway, Ollie said you attend university together?"

"He told you that?"

"Oh, sure. We talk once a week, he told me you were coming."

"Well, he didn't tell me," Jeanette mumbled.

"Hah! I told him you wouldn't like that. Ollie! She didn't like it!"

Oliver waved his hand from the makeshift bar where he was busy pouring wine and being corralled by his garrulous uncle again.

"So, what's your major?" Thomas asked.

"I'm working on my graduate degree in Art History."

"Ooooh, an historian," Marian intoned, leaving the 'h' out of the word entirely. "Did you see Aunt Adele's Rodin?"

"I did, it's a very good reproduction."

"Reproduction? Honey, it's very real. One of ten, I was told."

"Really?"

"Aunt Adele doesn't do anything halfway."

Thomas nodded solemnly.

Oliver returned with two glasses of white wine, Jeanette accepted one gratefully. Her head was swimming with this entire scenario. Was she at a family reunion? Why had Oliver brought her here? It wasn't as though they were dating. Oh lord, did he think they were dating? Jeanette took another slug of wine.

"How comes the writing, my dear?" Marian asked.

"Limping along at the moment, but better than blank pages," Oliver conceded. "What about you, how is the wide world of fashion?"

"Fashion won't market itself, I am busy busy in LA most of the season."

"And you're a semester away from graduating, Thomas?"

"I am, though father wants me to go for an MBA. I feel very done with school at the moment though. We can't all be the motivated academic like you, Ollie."

Oliver smiled, then turned to Jeanette. "Would you like to walk down to the water?"

She nodded.

"Let me refresh your drink, then we'll go."

She hadn't realized she'd finished it.

They descended the steps to the beach, passed the children still digging in the sand, and left their shoes behind. Jeanette felt her toes sink into the fine grains of warm sand, almost like walking along a firm, freshly baked cake. She left shuffling footprints as she walked, not wanting to separate herself from the earth, the only thing that felt real.

"So," Oliver began.

"So," she repeated.

"I told Marian about you. She thought it would be a good idea to bring you, she also said I should have told you, but I didn't want you to say no."

"I definitely would have said no."

"I figured."

They continued walking. The roar of the waves was louder now, it drowned out any superfluous sound and created instead a sphere of silence all their own. Jeanette could her his soft breathing, the shifting of the fabric on his shorts as he walked.

"Honestly, I just thought it would be fun. You could see the beach, eat some food, I thought you'd like Marian and Thomas…"

"Show off your nice beach house. I meant to ask, is this your second home? Or the primary one? Where do you store the servants? Is it an upstairs / downstairs kind of situation?"

Oliver scowled and mumbled, "It's our second house and we only have the one housekeeper. She's on vacation."

"Well, at least she's given that courtesy."

"Maybe this was a mistake."

Jeanette took a deep breath, followed by a sip of wine. "Oliver, you took me by surprise. I thought we were going to lay on towels, read a novel, maybe get a six pack of beer, I did not think we would be drinking white wine with your mom, sorry, mum."

"Yeah."

"Look, I appreciate your wanting to bring me. And your cousins *are* nice. So, I promise not to be a bitch, okay? Now can we please go wade into the water?"

He raised his head back up, the sheepish expression still vaguely present, a curl of hair fell across his forehead and his eyes looked particularly piercing in the sun.

Fuck, Jeanette thought.

But then he took her hand and they ran out toward the water together. The sun made the chill of the ocean dissipate almost immediately, Jeanette felt it pinking her back as she hiked up her dress and waded out further. The waves crashed a few feet in front of her and she let the tide push her forward and back, her feet suctioning into the ocean floor, becoming a part of it. Oliver was a peripheral creature when it came to the ocean.

Jeanette tried to remember the last time she'd stood in salt water. It had definitely been years, plural, since she had let herself be one with the sea. The ocean was a dangerous friend, too alluring. She'd spent much of her youth at the beach, hiding inside beach bungalows to read and cool off, then rushing back out into the waves again. She'd fallen in love with color there, the umbrellas, swimsuits, cabins, everything was neon, pastel, chromatic. It always felt like a rebirth after the frigid winter, and, with no one watching her, she felt doubly the freedom of youth.

Here, the sand was white, the ocean blue, Oliver's family decided neutral, but she felt that same magic again. It flowed from her toes to her fingertips and she let go of her dress's hem, allowing it to dip ungraciously into the water. She raised her arms up, closed her eyes, and let the wind take her secrets away.

Suddenly, Oliver was beside her.

"I didn't know if you could hear me," he said.

"I couldn't."

"You looked like you were enjoying yourself."

"I was."

He smiled. "Are you ready to go back to the house?"

"Only if you promise we can swim properly later."

"Deal."

Music was playing when they reached the threshold once more. The children had scattered and Adele was supervising the lighting of the grill, which another of Oliver's uncles attempting to accomplish to her exacting specifications.

"No, that's far too much charcoal!" She turned to them, "Did you two have fun?"

"We did," Oliver said, kissing her cheek.

"Mmhmm."

They wandered away from the ruckus to where Marian was playing patty cake with the two children.

"Whose kids are they?" Jeanette asked, for they seemed to belong to everyone.

"Mum's friend's daughter's kids, the grandmother watches them so she brought them along."

"Aren't they adorable?" Marian cooed, patting one on the head like a Cocker Spaniel.

Jeanette just smiled silently, essentially ignoring the children. "Is there more wine?"

Marian produced a bottle from thin air, "I've secreted this one away for a bit. I had to escape Uncle Bertie's ponderous story about his time at Oxford somehow, and if I couldn't do it physically..."

They settled in, with Oliver and Thomas, to chat about graduate courses, Marian's job in fashion marketing, Thomas's plans to move to New York, until Adele summoned everyone back to the deck for lobster tails. Marian tipped the rest of the wine into their glasses and, loosely stumbling a bit, they went to heed her call.

"We're not fancy here, don't stand on ceremony," Adele insisted as she handed out, what she referred to as, the 'everyday china' for them to eat on. "Everyone just mingle, no set table!"

Jeanette collected a lobster tail and some grilled asparagus before sitting down on the steps to eat. She wasn't going to risk the mistake of tipsy eating while standing and breaking any kind of china. That had to be nine years of bad luck or something, she thought.

Oliver joined her and they ate quietly, looking out at the ocean.

The lobster was so sweet she wanted to lick the plate clean, the asparagus she could do without.

"Not a fan?" Oliver asked.

"No."

He laughed, "Why did you get it?"

"I'd never had it before," she admitted.

A pause.

"Should we go swimming now?"

"I think you're supposed to wait thirty minutes after eating."

"It doesn't count if you ate seafood," he insisted.

"I am not sure that's a scientific fact."

"House rules."

"Can't argue with that."

They ran back out toward the water giggling like children. He pulled his shirt off over his head, exposing what Jeanette realized for the first time was a very firm physique coated with a fine down of dark hair. Jeanette gamely tossed her sundress aside in an act that surely scandalized Adele and dove headfirst into an oncoming wave. She emerged gasping, happy. Oliver swam up next to her and kissed her, the first time he'd done so on her mouth.

They broke apart and he was looking at her, about to say something.

The moment was broken by Marian, in a very chic one-piece, accompanied by Thomas, splashing toward them.

"Couldn't let you two have all the fun," Thomas laughed.

"I can't get my hair wet, it was just dyed," Marian insisted, which only provoked both boys to splash her relentlessly.

Jeanette put her head under water and filled her world with subtle movement and silence, a real world art installation. She pumped her arms and swam out past the breakers, just a head and shoulders bobbing in the glistening expanse. The sun began to set and Jeanette reluctantly emerged from her reverie, swimming toward the others, where they bobbed companionably together.

"We'll have to head back soon," Oliver said, letting the tide carry him to shore.

"Oh no! Well, maybe next time we will come see you," Marian offered, as she shook out her now thoroughly damp hair.

They walked back toward the house where four towels had been set out on the railing.

"Ah, Aunt Adele," Thomas muttered.

They toweled off, re-dressed themselves and went back in to say goodbye.

"Thank you for having me," Jeanette said to Adele.

"Of course, dear."

She turned to give a more effusive goodbye to Oliver, kissing him several times on the nose. "Don't work too hard, dear boy."

The drive back was quiet. Jeanette stared out the window, watching the sun set into the ocean. Maybe there was a little magic to the west after all.

Oliver parked in front of her apartment. "Thanks for coming today," he offered.

"It was fun. I actually did like Marian and Thomas."

"My instincts were correct, then."

"Not about everything."

"No," he smirked.

A pause.

"Do you want to come up?" she finally asked. She'd been thinking about it on the drive back, the moment he'd looked up at her on the beach. She'd known then she would ask him up.

His face lit up and he began to get out of the car.

She followed him upstairs, this man she knew and didn't know at all, wondering why he'd let her see the innermost part of him today. Maybe because she'd showed him the innermost part of her first. Jeanette opened the door to her apartment.

In moments, they were kissing. His mouth was warm, soft. Jeanette had never had a man back to her apartment before, but the futon mattress proved a quiet alternative to bedsprings. They lay together for a long time, touching but not having sex, until finally she asked the inevitable, "Do you have a condom?" He did.

Jeanette would consider later how what they had done was 'make love,' for lack of a better description. She was certain she wasn't in love with him, at least not entirely, but his sexual nature was slow, tender, and she came twice. He took his time and didn't rush her or himself. Afterward, they lay entwined together and Jeanette's last thought before she fell asleep was 'this is nice.'

◇

Oliver was gone in the morning, in his place was a note: *Had to go back to campus, you looked so peaceful I didn't want to wake you.*

Jeanette rolled over, she was accustomed to men being gone in the morning and only half expected to see Oliver again.

Naked, she walked to the kitchen and drank water from the tap. Coupled with the cool linoleum floor it staved off the heat she felt inside. She opened the refrigerator, it was mostly empty save a can of iced coffee and half used block of cheddar cheese. She opened the coffee and considered simply biting into the cheese, but resisted her baser instincts in favor of slicing it onto toast, which she melted in the oven. She smoked a cigarette while she waited. The cheese dripped from the rack, crusting at the bottom and burning to a blackened crisp that sent an acrid scent wafting toward the low ceiling.

The kitchen had a small window that looked out into the alleyway. It was mostly obscured by a telephone pole and metal grate, but Jeanette opened it to free some of the trapped smoke. Noisy garbage trucks clattered down the street and someone shouted words she couldn't hear, whisked away on the air before they ever arrived to her.

Yesterday already felt like a distant memory in the way that early summer days do. The sunny self-portraits that return momentarily in the haze of a vibrant nostalgia. To Jeanette, it was a Polaroid and she would pin it to the wall inside her heart.

Though summer began soon, Jeanette had no intention of going anywhere or exerting herself more than was absolutely necessary. She had submitted several more chapters of her thesis and they'd been met with only minor edits. She assured her supervising professor she fully intended to spend the summer buried in research, though they both probably knew she'd whip something together two weeks before the term began.

Jeanette did go to the library that weekend. She spent an entire day sitting in a carousel and drinking tiny cups of the free coffee they handed out downstairs. She used the headphones they saved for the music majors and listened to whatever she could find: operas, audiobooks, film soundtracks. She took breaks to smoke and get another paper cup of coffee. She watched students return stacks of ten or more books they'd hoarded in their dorm rooms over the course of a semester.

Everything seemed simple. Boredom loomed on the periphery, but never fully took hold. Was this contentment, she wondered.

Her final scholarship installment for the year, coupled with meager financial aid, was enough to make her briefly consider that she might need to get a job. However, having no requisite skills for any sort of employable work, she reconsidered this idea and reverted to her original plan of establishing an ascetic hermitage in the library's study room. If she got too skinny, Vihaan would feed her.

Eventually, Jeanette relinquished the headphones and went to check her school mailbox. A small black envelope was waiting for her. Her initial thought was "Oliver," but she instead found she had been invited to a summer kickoff party for faculty and students. She decided to go.

Jeanette had been walking slowly around the emptying campus, smoking cigarettes, when it struck her that she wanted to look nice for the party. She abandoned campus, headed for the part of town she felt most comfortable in, the part filled with secondhand shops, liquor stores, and a Dollar Tree. Luckily, the racks at Goodwill were once again flush with the discarded goods of fleeing college students. She slipped inside to browse the store for something interesting to wear.

She found a simple black sheath dress, something she actually imagined would be more suited to Marian than her, but when she tried it on in the dressing room, it fit. The structured look gave her a gravitas that her sundresses lacked. A bit more searching and she turned up some funky black and white clip on earrings and a pair of black sandals. The entire outfit looked like a sin, cost less than fifteen dollars, and Jeanette loved it.

That night she slid into her second skin and walked the few

blocks to the party. The air was still cool in the evening, but not cold enough for a jacket. She carried her nearly empty pocketbook as well.

The party itself was a subdued affair, something between a college bacchanal and the staid yuppiness of Oliver's family. Professors from the Arts department and graduate students mixed freely, drinking expensive whiskey, and discussing the all important question of what it all means. It was a bit too self-congratulatory for Jeanette's taste.

"When you really get to the heart of it, art criticism is just uninformed opinion masquerading as something interesting. They've never made art and so lack the insight to penetrate to the core of a form."

"Those who can do, those who can't..."

Jeanette walked away from the conversation.

Near the hors d'oeuvres a woman in a long dusty pink dress that she allowed to absently brush the ground picked at a round dish of caviar. Jeanette recognized her as one of the assistant ceramics professors. She wore a floral patterned turban atop her head that provided an extra few inches and a bohemian vibe, her neck was clad with chunky jewelry which Jeanette presumed, correctly, she had made herself.

"I hate this fucking faux fancy food," she muttered.

"Me too," Jeanette heard herself agree.

The woman's head snapped up. "Right? I mean, what happened to pigs in a blanket, Swedish meatballs, I don't know what an 'asparagus gratin' is."

"I just tried asparagus the other day," Jeanette laughed.

"Really?"

"Yep." She reached for the warm Prosecco and poured some into the scalloped plastic cups that were set out at irregular intervals for guests.

The professor just raised her eyebrows and returned to moving the caviar around in the dish again. Apparently her lack of asparagus knowledge was enough to deem her an outcast from somewhat polite society. She wandered off toward the open door that led to a yard, a huddled group of people, and the smell of marijuana.

"You want some?" a man, well, boy really, offered her a joint.

She just nodded, inhaled, held it, exhaled, took a sip of Prosecco, and repeated the process. She didn't cough. The man-boy coughed profusely.

"Are you okay?"

"Sure, sure. Sorry."

She shrugged and took the joint from him again.

Pleasantly high and buzzed from sparkling wine, Jeanette took a sleeve of water crackers off the table and ate them as she headed for the door. No one told her goodbye.

The night was cooler than before, but she felt tempted to strip off all of her clothes and open herself entirely to the night. The stars were alive with flickering heat just like her own heart.

At the entrance to her stairwell a shadow blocked her path, Jeanette jumped back, nearly dropping her pocketbook, now filled with loose crackers and crumbs.

"Who's there?" she shouted. "I've got a gun!"

"Woah, there. It's me, Oliver."

He emerged into the safety lighting of the parking lot and she considered how little good said lighting had done her in the actual event of a stranger lurking in her doorway.

"Oh, hi." She unselfconsciously resumed eating the crackers.

"Where were you?"

"I went to the Arts Department party."

"Really? You went to that?"

"I didn't have any other plans." She felt a little defensive suddenly, prickly about her decision. "Why?"

"It just didn't seem like your thing."

She scoffed. "How on earth would you know 'my thing'?"

He shrugged, donned the dumb sheepish look she had come to like.

"So?"

"So, what?"

"What are you doing here?"

"Oh, I just... I wanted to see you."

His honesty took her off guard in her altered state.

"Well, come on up. I am thirsty."

He walked up behind her. "You smell like weed, but you look quite fetching in that dress."

She laughed and opened the door, falling inside.

"I don't have any food," she said.

Oliver produced a plastic bag she hadn't noticed him carrying. Inside was a frozen pizza, a bottle of white wine, two bags of chips, and her favorite brand of cigarettes.

"My hero," she whispered, kissing his cheek. It was stubblier than the last time she'd pressed her cheek to his, she noticed.

He busied himself, readying their collegiate feast, while she put on a record and sprawled out on the futon mattress.

"Have you ever noticed that Humanities majors are pretentious fucks?"

Oliver laughed, "Have you noticed that we are both Humanities majors?"

"I am intentionally not excluding us."

"Well, in that case, yes."

She watched the ceiling fan spin slowly, smelled the leftover burning cheese from her earlier snack as Oliver preheated the oven for their pizza, she listened as he found the wine opener and brought two glasses, along with a bag of chips to the futon mattress. They sat cross-legged, like children at a picnic, knees touching and placed the chips between them. Jeanette balanced the wine on her right knee as she faced him.

"You have very handsome eyes," she announced suddenly.

"Thank you."

"They're like moss-covered rocks."

He smiled at her.

She knocked her wine glass over to cross the space between them and kiss him. He held her in his arms and she felt steadied, firm. He let her move down his collar bone, his stomach. He moaned as she went lower still. The record began to scratch and time stood still for a little while longer.

They burned the pizza.

◇

Summer moved slowly and Oliver became something of a fixture in Jeanette's life. He kept things moderately interesting and, though she felt it beneath the surface, did not openly judge her frugal life, nor did they make another sojourn to his beach estate.

They did meet up with Marian and Thomas for dinner at an Indian restaurant Jeanette had found on Vihaan's recommendation.

"How authentic," Marian commented.

One evening, Jeanette broke the lock that prevented apartment residents from accessing the roof. She and Oliver spent evenings lying on their backs, smoking, softly talking or not talking at all, the nights were so often clear they could count stars.

Jeanette spent a little more money perfecting her almost all black budget wardrobe. She wore chunky Doc Martens, slightly scuffed from a previous owner, with a black spaghetti strap dress. She let her hair grow long and dark and wavy down her back.

"You look like a proper art major," Oliver teased her.

She smiled, secretly agreeing with him.

Jeanette had no interest in going to Oliver's apartment, no interest in comparing her life to his. She liked the idea that they were two constellations, made up of entirely different parts, that had only touched due to the earth tilting far over on its axis. Eventually things would right themselves again and she had no intention of mourning the eventual loss. Not even with her copious black outfits, already so well suited to mourn.

Together, they established an orbit. They made love on her futon mattress, they drank at the same pub they had begun to refer to as 'theirs': "Meet me at our bar later."

Jeanette still spent plenty of time at the library, sometimes with Oliver, sometimes without. He was most often sequestered with the friends with whom he intended to start the much discussed online literary magazine, the whole thing still an unformed ghost.

Jeanette met his friends, or as Oliver called them: his colleagues, a few times. They wrote poetry about sunsets and breasts and living freely. They smoked both cigarettes and pot and wore blazers with elbow patches. They also spent too much time considering a name for 'the thing.'

"*Semi,* for semicolon and also, *you know,*" one of the less erudite young men suggested.

"*The White Whale.*"

"*Phantasmagoria.*"

"We can do better than that," Oliver encouraged them.

Jeanette sometimes lingered, conspicuously eavesdropping on their conversations, but most often she disappeared to listen to music or drink the free library lobby coffee in thimblefuls.

One night in July, Oliver knocked at her door, a television under his arm. He was illuminated by the safety lights like a blue-collar saint come to install electronic devices, moths dive bombed at his haloed head.

"Are you moving in?" she asked, amused.

"No, I just wanted to watch a movie, and I decided I wanted to watch it with you."

Jeanette opened the door and allowed him to set up this strange new appliance. They eventually just put it on the floor, for lack of a better space. They shared a bowl of popcorn that Jeanette topped with salt, pepper, and shaved parmesan cheese and watched movies that Oliver had rented at the grocery store. The TV itself remained there for the rest of the summer and Jeanette stopped resenting its imposition after a while.

On particularly hot days, she bought ice pops from Vihaan and sat quietly licking the saccharine sweetness then and there, lest they melt, like an impatient child, while he mostly ignored her. One day, she mentioned the appearance of her new TV and he lent her a Bollywood tape, one she hadn't seen before. Jeanette watched later that evening, sprawled across her mattress. Oliver, she'd found, did not appreciate the romantic sentiments of Bollywood and so she watched the movie alone.

Together, they watched action films, comedy, anything they could rent for free from the library, which included a lot of documentaries. They ate cheaply and made love often.

It was a comfortable summer romance and Jeanette enjoyed it as such.

Sometime in mid-July, Jeanette sat at one of her yellow topped barstools, she'd dragged it into the kitchen to blow smoke out of her window and into the alleyway. She wore a sports bra, underwear, and the white terrycloth robe she had stolen from the hotel almost a year ago. Peter briefly crossed her mind, then disappeared just as quickly. The vines from her scavenged houseplants draped generously down the windowsill, cascaded across the cracked floor, giving her kitchen a tropical feel. The hot summer air added to the overall effect.

It was in this moment that Jeanette decided she felt happy. The realization surprised her as she had long ago given up on the idea of happiness. Contentment, perhaps, but not happiness.

Such an abstract concept, what did it even mean?

She decided it meant this: summer, days that last until night, ice pops with Vihaan, operatic music pumped through rented library headphones, thrifted dresses, a stolen robe, regular sex, enough money for a pack of cigarettes, the plants she'd grown from cuttings, Scotch, art books and writing about them, Oliver, the ocean, a single tube of orange lipstick, bare feet on the cool linoleum, morning light in her apartment.

As she sat contemplating, she noted with amusement that her breasts and stomach seemed rounder lately. Oliver had been feeding her well and it showed. She rubbed her belly, her nipples, which felt a little tender.

Probably my period, she acknowledged.

Only, when had she last had her period?

She tried to count backwards, but came up empty.

Calm down, calm down. You just forgot, it's not a big deal.

A quick glance under the sink revealed she had not repurchased tampons in quite a while, which was troubling. Still, Jeanette reasoned that she and Oliver always used condoms. It was fine, she wasn't all that regular anyway.

She sat back down on the barstool, tapped her foot against the leg in a frantic tattoo. The cigarettes had lost their languid joy and the comfortably warm summer morning was making her sweat.

Jeanette dressed herself and headed out into the morning in search of a pregnancy test.

Not how I thought I would be spending the day, she considered.

Her stomach twisted in impossible knots as she speed-walked to the corner store. She couldn't go to Vihaan, she doubted he'd have any anyway, but made her way instead to the chain drugstore a few blocks away. The drugstore was near a college campus and kept themselves always stocked with condoms, lubricant, and pregnancy tests. Jeanette easily located a test and, pulling several crumpled dollars from her pocket, purchased it. The cashier looked at her for a moment with something akin to pity, but when Jeanette met her eyes they darted away.

Back at her apartment, she unfolded the accordion pages containing directions, warnings about inaccuracies and false positives, check it after five minutes, then don't check it again later, that she should drink water, but not so much water as to dilute the test, she could pee directly on the stick, or into a cup where she could insert the stick.

She tossed the directions aside and more or less positioned the stick underneath her, then peed, liquid spraying off, warming her hands.

Jeanette set the stick aside. She had no one to wait with her while she anticipated her future, no mother to scold her, no friend to hold her hand, and she definitely wasn't going to tell Oliver yet.

The world, which this morning had felt golden and possible, now felt entirely grey. Her apartment's low ceiling shrank even lower, the whole studio, a box, a cage. She tried to practice deep breathing techniques, something a therapist had taught her long ago, something she'd immediately discarded as nonessential in her practical life. Yet now, here she was, twenty-three, head between her legs, breathing measured gulps of air. The minutes took a year.

When Jeanette returned again to the bathroom, she eyed the pee stick like a grenade. She leaned in close and saw her future spelled out in a dark blue plus sign. She had two options, jump on the grenade and allow herself to explode in a million tiny particles, absenting herself entirely, or she could throw it as hard and as far away from her as she could.

She took the second test in the box, because sometimes a grenade is in fact a dud, but this one was live and the results were exactly the same.

No false positives here, she lamented.

When Oliver came over, she was laying on her back, splayed out on the futon mattress like the chalk drawing of a corpse. The room smelled of smoke and vomit, though she'd tried to wash most of that away. A half empty glass of Scotch sat next to her.

"Rough day?" he asked, his tone a touch too jovial, missing the mood entirely.

Jeanette did not raise her head or acknowledge his presence. He took off his shoes and left them by the door like he always did, then padded across the linoleum in his socks making a muffled shuffling sound. He knelt down, then flopped forward to join her on the mattress, she on her back, he on his stomach.

"What's up?" he asked again.

"Oliver..." her voice trailed off.

"Yes?"

With a momentous amount of effort, she pushed herself into a seated position. She looked into his eyes, his stupid, beautiful, forest green eyes. What would those eyes look like in a child's cherubic face underneath a halo of curls? Her guts churned again. From Scotch and nicotine and nerves. She burst from the futon to evacuate her stomach in the toilet once more.

When she emerged, Oliver was holding a glass of water and looking gravely concerned.

"You're sick," he said.

She took the water, sipped it. It was cool, it staid the burning inside of her, the infection.

"I'm not sick, Oliver. I'm pregnant."

Jeanette would never forget how his worried eyes went wide, then crinkled with something akin to pleasure.

PART TWO

Oliver sat with her for a long time, listening to her lament this momentary tragedy of her life.

"You can afford to pay for an abortion, right?" she asked.

"Yes," he whispered.

"Well, then it shouldn't be an issue. Or not for much longer anyway."

Oliver didn't respond.

"What," she'd finally asked, irritated by his silence.

"What about keeping it?" he finally asked.

Now was Jeanette's turn to be silent. She tried to imagine her life with a child in it, where would it even live in her tiny, unsuitable apartment? Would she and Oliver have to move in together, spend weekends with Adele at the beach, put their aspirations on hold? Most importantly, there was the distinct lack of money.

"Oliver," she began, "I can't afford it. I don't have a job, I barely scrape by. I can't afford more than half of the abortion. How would I even manage to take care of a child?"

It was the wrong tact to take because he immediately brightened. "If it's just money, I can handle that. I've got it covered, completely." He placed her hands in his, "I can take care of you."

Jeanette's heart melted a little. No one in her life had ever offered to take care of her before and, most often, she'd been alone. She'd cultivated a life built around loneliness in that way that others cultivate theirs to fit around a family. Jeanette had never considered 'family' as something positive, nor something she could ever really have for herself. Like 'happiness,' she wasn't even sure what the word meant to her at all.

"That's a sweet offer, Oliver, but..."

"Please," he said. "Just think about it."

"I've thought about it."

"I don't want to kill something that's a part of me, of you."

She cringed.

"She'll be beautiful and have your smile."

And your eyes, she thought.

"We can do this, together."

A week passed and Jeanette regarded her slightly rounded stomach as an intruder. Still, she began to slowly imagine what a family could be like. What it would be like to have someone who was always there, someone who didn't leave. The idea began to germinate into a possibility.

One afternoon, Jeanette sat on a bench at the park near her apartment. The expanse of green space offered an illusion of solitude, trees and bushes perfectly spaced to give park-goers leafy cubicles in which to hide themselves. Jeanette liked to spend particularly warm days under the shady trees, people-watching, and pretending to read a book. The heat of summer also brought families out in full force. Children played in the sprinklers and screamed as their parents chased them with towels. Couples lay on blankets picking at cold lunches they'd brought from somewhere else, that anointed place referred to as 'home.'

Directly across from her, Jeanette watched a mother, father, and child progress slowly along the paved sidewalk. The mother held the child's small hand on one side while the father held the opposite hand. Periodically, they'd lift their arms in tandem, pulling the child upward in a fit of giggles. The child, sandwiched in the middle, held both his arms up toward the tree trunks that were his parents, grasping them with the full weight of his body and the full force of assuredness that they would not drop him, ever.

It was this image, dappled by the summer sun, that Jeanette

held in her heart when she called Oliver from the park's payphone.

"Alright," she said. "Alright."

◇

When Jeanette had refused his initial offer to move in together, Oliver had instead insisted she reconnect her landline and the shrill ringing woke Jeanette a few mornings later from a dead sleep.

"Hello?" she grumbled into the receiver.

"Ollie just told me! Oh my god, Jeanette, I can't believe it! You and Ollie are going to make the cutest kiddo, I can hardly wait to meet them!" The voice was an effusive reminder of reality and Jeanette immediately resented the caller.

"Who is this?"

"Marian!"

"Oh, hi."

She went on and on about planning a baby shower, names, clothes, the best lotion to prevent stretch marks. Jeanette let the information wash over her like tepid bathwater. Marian seemed to have been long prepared for motherhood, thinking of things that Jeanette had hardly considered.

"Of course, no smoking or drinking or caffeine."

Of course.

"And you'll have to start taking more vitamins and feeding yourself properly."

Yes.

"What about you and Ollie? Well, don't even think about that right now."

I won't.

"And we can go maternity shopping! You're going to look so gorgeous pregnant! Not that you weren't already."

Ostensibly, Oliver would be willing to pay for pants to accommodate her rapidly expanding waistline, though Jeanette already mourned the loss of her chic sheath dresses. He would probably buy the vitamins too. She tried to stop tallying up expenses.

"I am going to come see you soon, and I imagine you'll come out here to alert Aunt Adele."

Adele.

"Ciao, darling! Kiss Ollie and baby for me!"

Jeanette hung up the phone, already exhausted before the day had even begun. People tend to forgive pregnant people exhaustion, didn't they? She hoped so, because she planned to take full advantage in the coming months. She also looked forward to riding in the handicapped seats on the bus, an accommodation in luxury that called out to her inner sloth.

Unfortunately, Marian had unintentionally presented an issue Jeanette still had yet to tackle, Oliver's grande damme of a mother.

"Will you tell your parents?" Oliver had asked her.

Jeanette had laughed in response, but she also hadn't asked if he planned to tell his own mother.

She picked up the phone and dialed his number.

"Hello?" he answered on the first ring.

"Oliver, did you tell Adele?"

"Of course," he chirped. "She wasn't exactly thrilled, but she'll come around. She loves having kids around, as you know, and she won't be able to resist ours."

"Well, then why wasn't she thrilled?"

He paused, she knew it was because she'd worn a ten dollar sundress and had never eaten asparagus.

"You know, parents. Plus she was taken aback," he pushed on. Jeanette appreciated his efforts.

Deep in her heart she tried to connect it to the heartbeat of her child to the heartbeat of family, their family.

"Are you busy today?"

She laughed, "No."

"Should I come over?"

"If you want, I'm extremely tired so don't expect to be entertained."

"You should just move in with me and I could take care of you."

Another pause.

"Come over whenever you have time."

They ate Chinese takeout, watched Tom Hanks dance on a keyboard, and Oliver didn't mention moving in together again. He did, however, present her with a plastic bag filled with vitamins, fresh mandarins, and a book on motherhood. She felt a surge of compassion for him then, he was trying. She ate one of the mandarins for desert and kissed him on the lips.

Later that night, after Oliver had gone, Jeanette stayed up trying to work on her thesis. The moon was bright outside her window and this leant a shadowy depth to the proceedings. Normally, she would have gotten up, paced for a while, smoked a cigarette. Now, she just paced.

Jeanette found that, without cigarettes and airplane bottles, she often had nothing to do with her hands. As a result, she began fidgeting, picking at her clothes and blankets, taking small balls of fluff and pilling them in between her fingers in an effort to distract herself. The leftover mandarin peels made the entire apartment smell like citrus rather than tobacco, which in turn began to make her nauseous. She chewed on straws, toothpicks, lollipops, Jolly Ranchers, ice cubes. She also found that her writing didn't flow when she was otherwise distracted. Jeanette wondered if the fetus was stoppering some of her writing, stealing her words through the umbilical cord.

Mostly, Jeanette used her restless evenings to thumb through her art books, a collection she'd been accumulating for a while. Many were textbooks she hadn't been able to to throw away, others were thrift store finds. Once used for her classes, she found herself seeking in them now a different education.

She looked at paintings of motherhood, mostly renderings of the Virgin Mary holding baby Jesus to her breast. Her face was often impassive, her eyes hooded, body hidden. El Greco painted her as little more than a child with cherubic lips, alabaster skin, and wide, dark eyes — this was a woman who held a secret. Although she felt a kinship in womanhood, there was an absence of tenderness under the inky oil impasto, a presence instead of simple duty and obedience behind dead eyes.

Appealing to her Surrealists, Jeanette looked at *Maman* by Louise Bourgeois, a monolithic spider sculpture, her soul sister, overblown in proportion, standing alone against a blue expanse of sky. The spider carried an egg sack containing thirty-two marble eggs. The sculpture, however, will never experience the bursting forth of life, instead she is doomed like Atlas to carry upon her thorax the burden of motherhood for all eternity.

The painting that most impressed upon Jeanette the dignity and caring often implicated in motherhood was *The Child's Bath* by Mary Cassatt. In the painting, a dark haired mother holds her child gently around the waist, a pudgy tummy exposed, then covered by a white sheet, then calves exposed again at the sheet's edge. The mother bathes her child's toes, while both their eyes are downcast, the child learning, the mother teaching, their expressions soft. Despite the inherent quiet in the painting, the accompanying room is filled with patterns, wallpaper, the pitcher, her dress, the rug. To Jeanette it seems like a cozy, safe place. The child's gender is ambiguous and Jeanette finds it easy to imagine herself as both mother and child.

This image, coupled with the family in the park, provides Jeanette with an interior painting all her own. She colors her world with soft eggshell, terra-cotta, sage green, she paints a home, a room like the one in Mary Cassatt's painting, a safe place. She adds a child of indeterminate features, she adds herself, and Oliver. She adds a simple meal at an already set table, she makes them all smile with a flick of her imaginary brush. The strokes are loose, impressionistic, not fully formed, but she's set the structure there and, with a few determined lines, it could all be filled in.

◇

Jeanette's classes were beginning again soon. She'd declined the offer to TA, and instead resolved to focus solely on her thesis writing. She signed up for three classes and an independent study. With luck, she could finish in just two more semesters.

Per usual, the onset of fall semester still felt like summer, all the ants returned to their ant hill clad in shorts and polos, sandals and dresses. Jeanette floated above them now, like a child's balloon, a single jostle could separate her connection from reality. The undergrads all seemed wholly formed, solid clay, while she felt more like dangerously fragile porcelain or the tiny glass animals from a Tennessee Williams play.

The new life she'd decided to carry changed her relationship to herself. It also made her focus sharp, crystal honed. She took notes in class, wrote essays, studied slides and glossy inserts from her art textbooks. She missed cigarettes and drank herbal tea instead. Everything was a mosaic of words, color, lectures.

One week after the semester started, she met Oliver at the library. She'd gone to the campus doctor that morning and he'd pronounced her healthy, but definitely still pregnant. They did an ultrasound and printed out the grainy black and white image for her, an inverse negative, a tiny bean that would become a human. Jeanette held the photo out to Oliver.

"Wow, it's so fascinating to see it up close. It feels both more and less real."

"You can keep it," Jeanette told him.

He smiled and placed it in the canvas cross body satchel he always wore on campus. He was TAing this semester and already had a stack of papers to grade. He would graduate in December, she felt certain no hindrance would prevent his matriculation. She wished this outcome for him, yet also envied it.

"I made plans to see mum this week, I'd really like for you to come with me."

"Sure, I can do that." Jeanette knew the experience of

confronting Adele needed to be quick, like pulling off a bandaid, and she preferred the discomfort sooner rather than later.

"We'll meet for dinner then, I'll pick you up."

She nodded.

He kissed her, deeply, on the lips. She kissed him back, surprised. They hadn't been particularly affectionate since the pregnancy. Jeanette suspected he was scared to have sex with her now because the fragility she'd conjured inside of her own mind somehow projected outwardly to him.

"I miss you," he whispered.

"Same," she smirked. "Hey, how's the lit mag coming along?"

"We decided to call it *Parabolas*. It was the path of least resistance. We bought the domain name and Travis is working on the layout in his graphic design class, so we should have something tangible in the next week or two."

"Just in time to prey on all the unsuspecting undergrads?"

"Exactly."

They parted ways, each headed to their own private world of academia.

Outwardly, not much had changed for either of them. She doubted, in fact, that Oliver had told any of his buddies he was an expecting father outside of the familial circuit. He could hide this part of himself for as long as he chose, though Jeanette knew she would not be able to hide her physical condition forever. Not that anyone would care, there were pregnant graduate students and professors on campus, she simply didn't want to attract any attention to herself. Her all-black ensembles and serious demeanor kept her off anyone's radar, they often mistook her for a shadow. She didn't want to become some well-meaning academic counselor's pet project.

The Adele dinner was set for Friday and Oliver arrived at her apartment dressed in a pressed button down shirt and pleated trousers. Jeanette had planned this time and looked equally smart in a dress, sandals, and a chunky necklace she'd bought at the campus art sale for ceramics students.

"So, where are we going?" she asked.

"I am honestly not sure, mum made the reservations."

"Ah," she replied.

He turned the radio on.

The restaurant was quite a drive from campus and exactly what Jeanette had expected, posh and modern. Oliver valeted the car and they ascended the white stairs, toward ostentatiously frosted glass doors. Oliver protectively took her arm as though to keep her from falling, but Jeanette sensed it was also a show of solidarity. They entered together, side by side.

Adele was already waiting for them at a round table dressed with white linen and too many pieces of silverware.

"Ollie," she stood and kissed his cheeks. She wore a tailored navy pantsuit with heels that Jeanette immediately took note of. Mother and son still stood locked in an embrace that consisted of Adele's outstretched arms touching Oliver's shoulders.

It seemed Jeanette would need to interject in order to ever actually eat dinner, and she was starving.

"Hello again," Jeanette offered her hand and Adele took it, shaking it limply. Oliver extricated himself and they all sat down.

A waiter approached to fill their water glasses while no one spoke.

Jeanette reached for a breadstick from the basket at the table's center and loudly crunched while mother and son enacted a silent showdown. She was accustomed to uncomfortable family dinners and could wait out most awkward silences with breadsticks, carbs were essential now that she wasn't allowing herself wine. The dining room was fairly crowded, mostly with older, impeccably dressed couples, women like Adele, and what looked like business associates, a plethora of men in black suits drinking Old Fashioneds and laughing a little too loudly.

Modern on the outside at least, Jeanette thought.

"How are your classes?" Adele ventured finally.

Jeanette admired her ability to forestall, though she docked Adele an imaginary point for being the first to speak.

"Good. I'm working as the teaching assistant for Professor Vaughn again and I've only got two more courses before I qualify for December graduation. Assuming I pass, I will have my degree then."

"You'll pass," Jeanette stated, smiling at him.

He smiled back, their camaraderie publicly sealed once more.

"And then what?" Adele pressed on, ignoring their exchange.

"And then I'll pursue my PhD and work on the literary magazine."

Silence descended upon the table once more like a thick woolen blanket. Jeanette clacked her teeth together to make sure she hadn't actually gone deaf.

The waiter reappeared to take their order.

"Watercress salad, dressing on the side, extra salmon," Adele ordered, crisp as a military sergeant.

"Chicken cacciatore for me," Oliver added, clearly accustomed to being the only plus one when dining with his mother.

"Lemon ricotta pasta, and more breadsticks please," Jeanette stated. She didn't mind that she'd ordered last, though the waiter looked clearly uncomfortable with their dynamic and beat a hasty retreat.

"That's all well and good, Oliver, but you know what I mean."

"No, mother. What do you mean?"

Jeanette readied herself for impact.

"What on earth are you going to do about this other situation?"

"Our child?" He took Jeanette's hand and Adele was forced to look at them both.

"Yes."

"We don't know yet," Jeanette replied.

Oliver squeezed her hand a little too tightly.

"I'm sorry?"

"We haven't made any plans."

A long pause while Adele drew in breath for the final assault.

"Clearly you don't plan, my dear. I am painfully aware of that.

However, as I see it, you have two options. You will either get married and move in together or you will get married and then move in with me so that I can oversee the child's care. You might not have a plan, but I've done this before and I'm not going to let a grandchild of mine grow up in some ragamuffin apartment in a bad part of town. You will make this situation suitable."

Adele's anger made her accent more pronounced and prevented Jeanette from understanding the entirety of her tirade, but she got the gist. Jeanette shot a quick look at Oliver who was no longer meeting her eyes. Adele had clearly won, despite her initial deficit.

"Mum, we will figure it out. And we appreciate your offer to help, of course. Jeanette and I are prepared to take full responsibility..."

Adele held up a manicured hand to stop him.

"Oliver, my dear, you have never worked. The trust pays for your college, your apartment, your little hobby magazine. Be realistic. If your father were still alive, he'd cut you off."

Oliver's face had turned red.

"Alas, I am unable to be that cruel."

"Let's just enjoy the food and a a nice evening together," Jeanette chirped. "Adele, would you like to be grandmère or grammy?" She intended to keep Oliver from saying something everyone would later regret. She, unfortunately, knew they would need Adele's help.

The waiter arrived on cue and placed their dinners in front of them. Oliver and Adele picked sullenly at their food while Jeanette consumed hers with relish, albeit while using the wrong fork, which no one noticed aside from Adele. She dipped another breadstick in the pasta sauce and felt satiated, solid again. An aperitif would have been the perfect accompaniment, or a cigarette, but she settled for filling the silence with mastication until Adele finally asked for the check.

◇

Each day Jeanette found it a little harder to roll herself off the futon mattress, so she'd lay there in the morning light as long as she could, cupping her hands to her gently rounding stomach.

The books Oliver gave her on pregnancy and motherhood told her she might not feel the initial bonding with her child until after it had been born. It took some mothers longer than others. Jeanette held out hope that she fit into the latter category, but mostly she just resented the fact that everything felt so much more difficult than it had a few months ago. She was constantly tired, constantly hungry, and smells were constantly making her nauseous.

Still, she imagined the bean swimming around an endless abyss, an entire secret world lived inside of her, like Frida Kahlo's *What I Saw in the Water*. She returned often to the public park and inserted herself into the mother role of various family vignettes. In this way Jeanette's imagined counterpart fed the ducks, tossed pennies in the fountain, and held hands with a partner who looked at her adoringly. She lived a thousand lives from that stationery bench and extrapolated from these moments her own pseudo-reality.

Marian came to visit. They met at a cafe, a popular place to bring parents visiting campus, and ate chicken salad sandwiches.

"How are you feeling?" Marian asked.

"Fine."

"Really?"

"No."

They each took a sip of bright pink passion fruit tea, the ice clinked against the glass.

"How's Ollie handling it?"

"I'm sure he's told you."

"I think he's always wanted to be a father. The absence of his own looms large you know."

Jeanette nodded, though she didn't really know.

"Heart attack at fifty-six is a rough way to go."

Jeanette used the iced tea as a placeholder once more.

"So, shall we go shopping?"

Jeanette had promised to take Marian to all the hidden vintage and thrift store gems that studded her college town and Marian promised to make Jeanette not look like a dowdy, pregnant frump.

The first place specialized in name brand resale and Marian practically screeched when she found a vintage Hermes scarf. They continued onward, Marian ever more laden with accessories. At the last place, Jeannette bought a couple of billowing black dresses, the kind that may have once graced a Fleetwood Mac performance, and decided such a silhouette could be utilized when the time came. Her closet was filled with primarily unstructured things that would still work for a while. Who knew pregnancy would require so much sartorial forethought, she considered.

They walked past a boutique baby store Jeanette usually avoided making eye contact with. Marian insisted on purchasing something.

"Look! This jewelry is made from silicone and you can wear it while the baby is teething."

Jeanette cringed, the idea of wearing jewelry covered in dried saliva did not appeal to her.

Marian moved onward, "What about this?" She held up a stuffed elephant which Jeanette admitted was quite cute. The women parted ways with the false calls of, "We simply must do this again soon!"

Back at her apartment, she tossed the elephant into her back closet before collapsing in a heap on the mattress once more.

Jeanette made it through the semester, she passed her classes and submitted an almost completed thesis on female Surrealism with an added emphasis on the depiction of motherhood. Her professor described it as 'astute.'

Oliver graduated. Jeanette sat in the front row clutching the program, smiling, even though her back ached from sitting in the metal folding chair. He beamed as he accepted his degree, shook the dean's hand.

Watching him cross the stage, his head held high, she was suddenly called back to the night before, remembering how they'd made love, slowly and carefully, avoiding too much jostling.

"I don't want to hurt the baby," he whispered.

"You won't," she assured him.

He'd left early that morning to get ready for the ceremony, self-assured, a man who had map of his future. Jeanette found herself almost believing in the same plan herself.

Adele sat next to her, graceful despite the folding chair, staring straight ahead, a thin smile drawn across her painted lips.

Afterward, they all embraced, took photos.

Parabolas had also published its inaugural edition of poetry, prose, and hybrid art a few weeks prior. Oliver's name and photo sat proudly under the 'masthead' link on the website dutifully, and professionally, designed by his friend. Professors had approached Oliver to congratulate him on starting something new from scratch, they praised the quality and his vision.

"Everything is going to be okay now," Oliver whispered into her hair before he rushed off into the throng of people to meet his fellow graduates, his compatriot conquerors of the universe.

While Oliver went out to celebrate, Jeanette, though she desperately longed for a swig of something strong and a cigarette, or a pack of cigarettes, declined, knowing she would break under the temptation. She had surreptitiously smoked half a pack over the course of her pregnancy, a secret she decried to no one. But she could hardly be seen purchasing them now, in her advanced state. She knew Vihaan wouldn't even sell them to her.

Those cigarettes were the first thing she thought of when she woke up in the night with a searing pain in her abdomen. She cried out, but no one was there to hear her. Blood stained her underwear, the sheets.

Jeanette crawled to the landline and called Oliver. There was no answer at his apartment.

Her second call was to a taxi service, a frightened man helped her into the car, then ferried her to the hospital. She put on several more pairs of underwear before leaving so as not to stain his seat.

"Don't you need an ambulance? A doctor?"

"Can't... afford it," Jeanette informed him, through clenched teeth.

At the hospital he helped her to the door, then made a quick escape. She didn't blame him. One of the nurses spotted her clutching her stomach and admitted her immediately.

Alone, in a pale blue hospital gown, the doctor explained to Jeanette her current predicament.

"You have a thin placenta lining. Any extreme movement, really any movement, could cause a miscarriage."

Jeanette nodded her head.

"You'll have to be on bedrest for the next two months."

"Two months? But, I'm on track to finish my graduate degree, I need to go to class."

"You'll have to take a semester off."

She could, she knew she could, she knew the college would allow her due to 'extenuating circumstance.' Her body felt again like easily breakable porcelain.

"No, I can't do that."

"This is very important for both your health and the health of the baby, you could both die. And you'll have to stay overnight. You've lost some blood and we'd like to give you a fluids IV and monitor your progress to make sure it's nothing more serious. Totally routine," the doctor assured her before exiting the room.

A worried nurse hovered, making Jeanette increasingly uncomfortable.

"Is there anything I can do?" she asked.

Jeanette wrote down Oliver's number, handed it to the nurse, then allowed herself to surrender entirely to sleep.

The morning light was muted by gauzy window dressings, long ago conceived of as something to brighten the room, now, yellowed with age and use, they'd been parted to allow morning sun in. This, coupled with the shivering fluorescent bulbs overhead, lent a sickly yellow tinge to the room. Everything looked jaundiced. Jeanette's knees were covered with a pastel blue blanket at the foot of her bed, she still wore the blue hospital gown.

In a chair, next to her bed, slept a grizzled Oliver. His face was grey and stubble dotted his chin. He wore the clothes he'd graduated in, but now the tie hung loosely around his neck.

He was here though, he had come. She hadn't known if he would.

Jeanette's heart surged with such tenderness toward him that she reached out to touch the stubble on his face, let her fingers softly trace his eyebrows. His eyes flicked open.

"Hi," she said.

"Oh god, Jeanette! I'm so sorry. They called me so late last night, I thought the worst..."

"Shh, everything's fine."

She cradled his hand and lifted it to her cheek. They stayed there, frozen in that position, until the nurse came to bring Jeanette a light breakfast of yogurt and granola. She wondered what kind of portrait a Renaissance painter might glean from this particular tableau, the symbolism of granola.

"The doctor says you're good to go home today. They told me about the bedrest thing," Oliver added.

"Yes, damn inconvenient."

He took a deep breath, then began his obviously prepared speech.

"I know you value your independence, Jeanette. I've tried to be respectful of your space, I always go to your apartment in penance for my not immediately loving it. But you are going to have to come live with me, let me take care of you, and the baby."

"I have to take a semester off," she responded.

"Lots of people do that."

"How many go back?" she asked, looking directly at him.

He shrugged, "If anyone can buck a statistic, it's you."

It was the correct answer and she let him take her back to his apartment. As she had gleaned from previous conversations, it was located in a part of town she rarely spent any time in. The neighborhood was littered with natural grocery stores and couples walking tiny dogs. His apartment was on the top floor of a three story building and, of course, there was an elevator. She tried not to point out this decadence in a condescending way as it would clearly come in handy for her in the future.

The apartment itself was a learned man's haven. His living room had a leather sofa and matching club chair, a very large globe for some reason, several shelves of books, and several bottles of very expensive whiskey. He had two bedrooms, which immediately annoyed her. One was obviously where he wrote, a desk overflowing with papers, a charging laptop computer hummed on top of them. The other had a well-appointed king-size bed on a bed frame that raised it almost three feet above the ground, an unaccustomed treat.

"I hate your apartment," she said, as he helped to deposit her in the bed.

Oliver just laughed.

He was good to his word though and, over the next two weeks, did help her in every way he could. He brought things over from her old apartment in a truck he borrowed from one of his *Parabola* colleagues, stored them in a large walk-in closet. He placed her laptop nearby so she could work on her essays for class, then turned her finals in for her, with a doctor's note, helped her communicate the situation to the registrar's office. He took her last month of rent and key in an envelope to Jeanette's landlord.

She was, in a word, ensconced, a queen trapped in her tower. Quietly, she mourned the loss of her studio, that she hadn't gotten to give it a proper goodbye, that she hadn't had a chance to swim in the kidney-shaped pool once more.

Jeanette made a point of resisting the creature comforts Oliver was able to provide, accustomed to privation, the mantle of the bourgeois did not sit easily upon her shoulders. Oliver kept a running commentary about the best foods for her to eat, iron-rich, and turning the second bedroom into a nursery. He even went so far as to purchase a crib, or perhaps Adele purchased it. Either way, it was assembled in the bedroom they now shared when he didn't spend the nights in his office writing.

Oliver, it turned out, was gone most of the day, he had decided to take a part-time adjunct position at the college and lingered on campus in the computer lab, working on the literary magazine or preparing his lectures. He needed space to think, he said. She understood and left him to it. He always made sure she had things within reach.

The doctor-imposed rest was initially a true cure for her exhausted physical body. She was able to lay very still and watch the sun move from one end of the room to the other. Jeanette became acutely aware of the time of day in relation to the sun, like an old sailor. She let her limbs sink heavily into the sheets. They smelled of lavender laundry detergent, the kind Oliver liked. He had a housekeeper who came once a week to do laundry and clean the house.

During the second week of her confinement, which she'd taken to calling it after reading a historical fiction set in Tudor times, she'd run out of things to read and had begun to pick apart pieces of tissue paper out of boredom, she asked Oliver to pick up some art supplies.

"Just a few things, when you have time. A sketchbook, pencils, paint, paintbrushes?" She listed items at random, in the order of priority in which they appeared in her head.

It was an impulsive thing, but something in her stirred with the need to create. She wanted to run her hands along the petals of a flower and then replicate it on the page. Art could be learned, all she needed was time, and she presently had that in spades.

Oliver indulged her request and returned with watercolors, oils, and an easel in addition.

The materials were an unexpected abundance and she stared at them, the colors in their plastic tubes and cellophane wrappers. They were a rainbow-hued challenge and a solution to her idle hands.

Jeanette balanced the sketchbook on her stomach and one of her *Theory of Art* textbooks next to her. The king-sized bed gave her space to move about and she soon established an artist's residence of sorts, the easel she set up next to the bed so she could access it while still sitting on the edge of the mattress. Jeanette began, as suggested, with gestural sketches, rushed memories of an object, then contiguous lines, over and over until she could draw a pair of interconnected hands with her eyes closed. She set up small still life studies in the bedroom and drew them, one line then another, until she had something. Her sketchbook filled up with toothbrushes, lamps, stacks of books. Then she got creative and tossed a throw over a nightstand, arranged some fruit, made it look lush. She spent hours perfecting folds with her pencil, not noticing the sun had sunk below the horizon. She sat on the floor in front of the floor length mirror that hung on the inside of the closet door and drew her own face. This had the added effect of allowing her to truly appreciate her own nose for the first time.

Jeanette filled up an entire sketchbook and requested another one. She taped some of her sketches to the easel and scooted to the edge of the bed to begin her first attempts at painting. Staring at Van Gogh doesn't make someone an oil painter, that was her first lesson. The second was that she needed to put a towel on the ground to protect Oliver's hardwood floor and security deposit.

Slowly, she began to blend colors onto a palette, her initial muddy browns gave way eventually to more subtle burnt umber and auburn. She painted bright orange mandarins in a wooden bowl, the ones Oliver insisted she eat as though she might get scurvy. Although, with her luck, it might happen. She set the bowl atop a red blanket Adele had given them as a housewarming present. "I had it lying around and wasn't using it," she'd said, by way of presenting it. Now, it was the backdrop for Jeanette's first true still life painting. She spent time dimpling the skin of the mandarins, adding cast shadows to the bowl, attempting a wood grain pattern for depth, as she'd already perfected folds. Then, she filled in the background with a dark grey that faded to black in the light of the setting sun or reflecting the dimness she felt inside her own head, her inner world burning brighter with each dark brush stroke.

When Oliver came home that night, his arms loaded down with papers, he paused in the doorway. Jeanette was still staring at the painting, one hand gripping her brush, the other laid gently across her stomach.

"That's kind of extraordinary," he said. Then, he kissed her on the forehead and retreated to grade the essays.

Jeanette sat still, in disbelief that she had created something so close to perfect.

Her next creation was something significantly more visceral.

Jeanette's legs were splayed open and a team of doctors and nurses hovered over her vagina, measuring dilation, describing the baby's positioning. She felt certain this was what an alien probe felt like. Though she'd agreed to an epidural hours ago and had lost all feeling in the lower half of her body, she was also cut in half with a medical sheet like a magician's assistant. It lent a sinister aura to the proceedings.

"Okay, Mommy. It's time to push," the doctor said.

Mommy, it echoed in her ears. She felt dizzy with exhaustion and the concept of 'Mommy' suddenly seemed as foreign to her as Rome. Why hadn't she ever been to Rome?

And so began a very long and very sweaty exertion, until the baby was out and she'd shit herself.

That was essentially all she remembered, moments of screaming and pain and telling a visibly frightened Oliver that she hated him, banishing him to the hallway. The baby was ripped from her like something out of a horror movie and, still covered in a bit of her own gore, they laid the creature on her chest. Her breasts were hard with milk and she resented their martyrdom to their new cause.

It was a boy. They'd waited to discover. His tiny penis looked like the tip of a flesh-colored green bean, but she counted ten fingers and toes, and he squirmed with life.

He was misshapen, grayish, nothing like her vibrant paintings.

Below the sheet, her body was being cleaned up, stitched back together, like Frankenstein's monster.

"What should we name him?" Oliver whispered to her, leaning over the child with transfixed awe.

"You choose," she'd replied, before falling asleep from the drugs and exertion.

She woke to Adele holding a cleaned and swaddled baby, whispering "Albie," in his ear.

"Oh, you're awake. Good. He needs to eat," Adele thrust the bundle at her, it was struggling against the swaddle, making the ungh-ungh sound that prefaced crying in newborns.

Groggily, Jeanette undid her night gown and pressed the baby to her chest. His mouth found her nipple with little effort and he began to suck and pull at her greedily. Jeanette winced in pain as his toothless gums clamped down, though it relieved the heavy feeling in her chest, she felt like a cow.

"It hurts," she complained.

Adele ignored her.

A nurse entered, "Oh, good! I was coming in to see if you needed help, but he looks like a good latcher."

"It hurts," she repeated.

"It can, but the pain lessens over time."

Jeanette unhooked the baby from her breast, milk leaked onto the sheets, and he immediately began to cry, a keening wail that startled everyone.

"No. I can't," Jeanette stated.

The nurse looked sympathetic.

"You have to feed Albie, it's your duty as a mother," Adele stated, her protestation mostly drowned out by the baby's cries.

"I will. I just think we will both prefer formula."

The nurse nodded and went to make up a bottle.

The vein near Adele's temple throbbed. An unattractive quality, Jeanette thought.

They brought Albert, that was what Oliver had named him, home the following morning. Adele had offered to stay with them for a couple of weeks, to help, but Jeanette had passed on the idea.

"Clearly, you will need help," she insisted.

Eventually, Adele and Oliver came to the bargained conclusion that, in addition to their housekeeper, Adele would employ a nanny two days a week. It felt more like Adele assigning a prison guard to watch over her, but Jeanette was free now, a creature of malleable clay upon the earth.

Oliver sat with the baby on his lap in the morning while he read the paper, ate eggs, then passed Albert off to Jeanette or the nanny before heading out to work, offering him a quick pat on the head.

Jeanette did not crave time with Albert as she had expected she might. Instead, he seemed to create a tiny forcefield around his body preventing her from getting close to him. She fed him bottles, burped him, bathed him in a sort of fugue state for the first few weeks.

She stopped noticing Oliver's comings and goings, stopped responding when he asked her a question. In the evenings, when he was home, she ignored the baby and Oliver entirely, feeling herself sink beneath the loam, into a constricted silence. Oliver stopped talking to her, turning his conversations to baby chatter, a noise that drilled into her skull until she shouted, "Please, be quiet," from the back room. She heard the door shut and knew they'd gone out together.

"Jeanette," he said her name softly at first, then more insistently, then not at all. For a while, she didn't notice he'd started sleeping on the couch. Their bed was left cold as Oliver wouldn't sleep in it and Jeanette wandered through the apartment like a lost spirit. Her imagined family portrait had fractured at some point and she didn't have the energy to try putting it back together.

Only on the days when the nanny arrived, when she began forcing herself to leave the house, did she understand herself again. Her particular voice returned to the empty places inside her mind. It was winter now, and the world was crisp, the sky blue. Jeanette ambled pointlessly, then began walking back to her old neighborhood, at least two miles. Her body strained at the exertion, but she pressed on, lingered in the parking lot of her old apartment building, looking up at her old window, and feeling as though she'd lost a loved one.

She walked to the corner store. Vihaan turned and his eyes lit up when he saw her.

"It's you," he said.

"It's me."

He patted her on the shoulder and they watched part of a soccer match, Jeanette didn't know either team, but she needed this puzzle piece of her old life. He sold her cigarettes, a few airplane bottles of Scotch. Now that she was no longer visibly pregnant, he could hardly reject her request. He also gave her a packet of Indian milk candy as she left.

"Come back," he said. "Bring baby photos."

She smiled and nodded.

Outside the air was fresh and a cool breeze whipped under the scarf she was wearing. She still had on one of her maternity dresses. Adele had pressed her to breastfeed again and again, assuring her she would lose the 'baby weight,' but Jeanette stood firm. Now, her breasts were empty of milk and her own again.

She lit her first cigarette in months, inhaled, her mouth an 'o,' a moan escaping with the exhale. Her whole head felt dizzy and she tilted it back to laugh at the sky. She finished one cigarette and lit another, opened a bottle of Scotch. The alcohol burned and warmed the back of her throat pleasantly, warding off any chill. Mixed with the nicotine, it was the perfect cocktail.

She walked along the sidewalk where she once wore sundresses and sandals and felt contentment, now she was a lurching, overweight mom, drinking straight liquor, and laughing to herself. In her billowing dress and oversized scarf, she could easily be mistaken for a bum. This thought made Jeanette burst into fresh peals of laughter.

Oliver came home late and she was bathing Albert in the sink, he'd shit himself again.

"It smells terrible in here," Oliver complained.

She indicated the shit covered baby in the sink and shrugged in response.

"No." He sniffed her. "It's you. You've been smoking."

"So?"

"What do you mean, 'so'? That's not setting a very good example for Albert."

"Oliver, Albert does not give two shits about whether I smoke or not."

"You're a mother now," he continued.

"You're a father, why don't you come wash the shit covered baby in the sink and I'll go hide out in the office?"

Oliver glowered in a way Jeanette had never witnessed before, perhaps it was a latent skill he'd learned from Adele. He had that same throbbing temple vein and his new, short-cropped hair did nothing to conceal it. When he realized she wasn't going to pursue the argument further, he retreated to his study. He'd told her several times that his extra hours were for *Parabolas*'s sophomore attempt. Now that the site possessed some cachet, they'd been adding it to forums, webrings, seeking a wider net.

"Oliver is being a little touchy this evening," she explained to the baby. Jeanette loathed baby-talk, would not refer to herself as 'mommy,' or the baby 'Albie.' She spoke in the same measured voice she used with all adults and, as far as she could tell, it was just another thing Albert didn't care about. He flung his arms up and down, splashing water and gurgling. Jeanette silently counted down the hours until the nanny would arrive: twelve, eleven…

The next time she had earned the key to her release through Adele's insistence of indentured servitude, Jeanette took her sketchbook. She sat in the park drawing, avoiding children and families, she drew women. Sometimes they happened to be mothers, sometimes they were joggers, or, like her, sitting in the park and having a private moment.

And this was how the days passed for her. She cared for Albert, played with him as she would any animal to develop his cognitive abilities, spoke to him in full sentences. Sometimes she had a cigarette on the fire escape while he played in a bouncing contraption that made him momentarily static. She had dinners with Oliver where she listened to him speak of a world that no longer existed for her, a world of books, thoughts, and interesting people. Was she an interesting person? Did he count her among them? Then, they put Albert to bed, sometimes had sex or shared a bottle of wine. He'd gotten over his initial aversion to her cigarettes and very occasionally joined her on the fire escape. On Mondays and Fridays the housekeeper came. On Tuesdays and Thursdays, the nanny. Adele stopped by whenever she felt like it, she was paying for the apartment after all.

Jeanette used all of her free time to draw and paint, keeping her hands busy. Most of the nanny days, she also walked the two miles back to her old neighborhood. She brought Vihaan baby photos, he gave her chai tea. Sometimes she sketched things in Vihaan's store, sometimes she brought watercolors to the park. She proved Adele wrong by walking and smoking the baby weight away. She changed back into her black dresses, went to the hairdresser and cut her dark hair into a fringed bob, wore terracotta orange lipstick every day.

"You look like a Halloween costume," Adele told her.

Jeanette didn't respond.

One night she overheard Adele whispering furtively to Oliver in the kitchen.

"Where is her own family? Her friends? Why is she always here all alone with just her colors?"

"She doesn't talk about her parents, mum. I think they're dead."

"You think?"

"And all of her friends were back at school. Since she dropped out, she doesn't know any other moms."

Adele huffed. "Well you need to do something, Ollie, before she drops out of everything."

"What do you mean?"

The rest was so quiet Jeanette could no longer discern what they were saying. She smoked a cigarette in his office out of spite.

Several months after the first issue of Parabolas, Oliver and his co-editors released a second online edition. It had been universally decided they would publish quarterly from then on out. Jeanette lay in bed scrolling through the site. The writing wasn't bad, with the exception of one collection of exceedingly melancholic undergraduate poetry that went against the magazine's underlying tone. She checked the author, someone named Sofi Tremmel, a grainy black and white photo accompanied her bio: undergrad, lit major, very pretty. That explained it then, Jeanette thought, closing the laptop.

Jeanette had a momentary pang of jealousy for Sofi Tremmel, recalling her own essay that had gotten her the golden ticket graduate scholarship out west. The words flickered dimly in her mind, then dissipated. And what had she done with it? She felt disgusted with herself, with her gilded cage.

Their living area was lined with her oil paintings, slowly drying in the spring air. All the windows were open and Albert had woken, he was babbling happily. She picked him up, changed him, fed him, burped him, returned him to the crib, then she opened the magazine's home page again. Well, the difference was not that Sofi was younger or prettier than her, it was that she was out there submitting her work, Jeanette realized. What if I submitted my paintings to something? There had to be amateur art shows. An idea germinated.

They'd only gotten internet hooked up in their apartment recently. Oliver had deemed it a 'necessity' now that he had a burgeoning online editorial career. Wired to the wall, Jeanette pulled her laptop to the end of the bed.

Some initial searching led her to a bare bones forum listing several monthly or bi-monthly art shows in the area. She excluded herself from the ones that occurred on campus, she couldn't bear facing her former professors who spent their lives critiquing others' art and presenting her own meager attempts for their critical gaze.

Jeanette paced into the living room, past the crib where Albert slept on unaware a storm was brewing. She counted the paintings, twenty that were done, five that she considered decent. She returned to the computer and fired off an email to a local coffee house offering up a 'new artist's night: featuring an evening of open mic, artwork, and coffee!'

A response came later that evening, she would need to bring her work by for appraisal before she could be accepted to the show. This seemed fair, Jeanette considered. When Oliver came home, frazzled and flustered about grades being due and his adjuncting schedule the following semester, Jeanette decided not to mention her artistic plans. She whispered them in Albert's ear after he had fallen asleep.

Oliver tolerated her art in the same way he tolerated her smoking, which was to say: barely.

"It's a mess in here," he commented, regarding the state of the living room.

"It's not a mess, it's just cluttered."

"Same thing."

"I should hope not, we're paying a housekeeper."

He scowled.

"Don't worry, I will get rid of some of them soon." She kissed his head to placate him and went to open another bottle of wine.

A few days later, when the nanny was watching a petulant Albert, Jeanette donned one of her characteristic black dresses and lugged five canvases under her arm to be appraised by the coffee shop aficionados. They ultimately chose two: a dark study involving a vase of dead flowers set atop Adele's red blanket, it had a Vermeer quality she was fond of, and a large painting of a very small window showing the spring leaves outside as though from a great distance. She left these two at the coffee shop with an index card including her name and the price she'd charge for each piece, jokingly Jeanette priced them both at two hundred dollars.

It was around this time that Albert started constantly screaming. He screamed in the morning when he woke, when she tried to put him down for bed, randomly in the night. Every time, Jeanette rose blearily and tried to discern the issue, feeding, changing, usually failing, then drinking black coffee until he fell back asleep. Oliver, more and more often, stayed behind his closed office door and pretended he wasn't aware of the commotion, or stayed working so late, he'd miss the baby's bedtime entirely.

Jeanette stopped sleeping or making time to eat. Their housekeeper tried to ply her with food. Her name was Veronika and she clearly felt uncomfortable watching Jeanette wander around the house like a cross between Kate Moss and Hunter S. Thompson, robe open to expose her underwear, cigarette hanging off her lips. They didn't speak much, but Jeanette appreciated her concern.

Sometimes she would tune out the cry-screaming, the way someone might a ceaselessly ringing telephone, only coming to herself again when it was suddenly, unexpectedly silent. Then, of course, she immediately worried that Albert had somehow died, which was never the case.

The nights came sooner and Jeanette felt claustrophobic in the darkness.

When the evening of her art show loomed near, she asked Oliver to watch Albert for a couple of hours.

"Where are you going?"

"To an art opening," she answered honestly.

"Why can't you bring him?"

"Oh, come on Oliver. You know how those things are, he won't be entertained and I will have to leave without seeing anything. You've been working on *Parabolas* nonstop and I haven't complained, I just want one evening."

"Fine," he agreed. "What time will you be back?"

"Around eight or nine." She pulled him close and kissed his cheek, "Thank you, my darling."

She felt him physically draw away and dropped her hand from his shoulder. He had never resisted her, admittedly sporadic, affectionate caresses before.

"What's wrong?" she asked.

"Nothing," his voice was softer now. "Just stressed."

She placed her hand in the space between the shoulder blades on his back and felt him relax into her touch. They stood that way for a moment, until Albert started crying again.

The night of her show, Jeanette dabbed a bit of perfume on her neck from a rollerball she'd been saving since undergrad, donned her uniform of black and a sharp smear of deep orange on her lips, checked on Albert and Oliver, watching television together in the living room, then headed out into the balmy evening.

She walked slowly, picking her way down the avenues. Jeanette felt lighter than she had in months. The alternate reality was the one in which she had given birth, this was where she belonged.

At the coffee house, people spilled out onto the sidewalks. Everyone looked exactly how a group of artists at a coffee house should look, there were a lot of scarves and Chelsea boots, Jeanette blended in seamlessly. A hand printed pamphlet, essentially a piece of computer paper folded in half, listed the artists and writers alongside the titles of their works. It was the first time she'd seen her name in print next to the word 'artist.' Bottles of red wine were uncorked and set out next to clear plastic cups, an open invitation. She pulled the cork on a Merlot, poured a glass, and began to mingle.

The art works were all hung together on a wide, white wall, grouped by artist with accompanying index card underneath. There were mostly paintings, some watercolors and mixed media pieces, a couple of sketches in oil pastels, they were all of a generic 'good' quality, she thought. Jeanette particularly liked a small cluster of cityscapes, the use of monochromatic colored pencils, mixed with oil paint backdrops, created an interesting juxtaposition of the tangible nature in a city and the ability to feel penciled in, two-dimensional, a sketch of a real person. The rest, were interesting, but didn't draw further personal critique from her. Jeanette's paintings were among the largest and certainly the darkest, her colorscape seemed to drain all other colors to it, creating a deep violet darkness behind the dead flowers. She approved.

Leaning in, she saw underneath the vase of flowers, her index card had a red stamp: "Sold." She scanned the wall, there were no other stamped cards. Was someone playing an elaborate joke on her?

She panicked, found the coffeehouse curator.

"Oh, yes. Someone came in at the beginning of the evening. He said he was certain this one would go and paid cash. We don't take a percentage," she explained, expecting that was the source of Jeanette's concern, "It's all yours at the end of the show."

"Of course, thank you."

"You've already had a great start, enjoy the evening! I will find you later to sort the money and plan for the next event."

The next show.

Her plastic glass gleamed with rubies of leftover liquid and a perfect imprint of her lips, she went to the bar for a refill.

An open mic event was being set up. Someone had an acoustic guitar, but most of the artists appeared to be writers, poets, ready to take on the night with their words.

Jeanette appraised her paintings once more, then walked outside to smoke a cigarette. Everything felt very purple to her and she was happy to be alive.

The smoking area is where most artistic conversations take place, not perusing the actual art. One must observe, then quietly extricate oneself to a buzzing haze of nicotine where, under a streetlight, one's observations will appear infinitely more profound.

She stood on the periphery, listening.

"I mean, we all know New York is where you really want to go, to be taken seriously."

"That's such a misrepresentation of art culture."

"You think the people here intend to be taken seriously?"

"I think some of them do, yes."

"Then they shouldn't be here."

Jeanette considered this exchange as she smoked and drank her warm Merlot. Could artists be taken seriously in a location displaced from the 'scene'? She considered the 'outsider artists' movement, those creators, never formally trained, apart from the conceptual world, and often discovered posthumously. They made art for the pure joy of putting paint on paper, the physical pleasure of creation. Jeanette's own art was based on academic studies, not studio classes, she wasn't sure she qualified for outsider status. But there was something in her that called out, and seeing her art on the wall of a coffeehouse, while not a Paris salon, had awoken it. She didn't want to be discovered only after her death.

She lingered for another hour, talking to a few other artists, listening to poetry about a woman's first menstruation. 10PM arrived, and she decided it was time to return home. Like Cinderella after the ball, she left behind her lipstick on cigarette butts and plastic cups, a princess no longer.

She never did find out who bought her painting, but the money felt good in the pocket of her dress.

Albert was asleep and Oliver sat in the leather club chair, a Scotch in one hand, a book he clearly wasn't reading in the other.

"Did you two have fun?" she joked, kicking her shoes off in the doorway.

"Not particularly. It was hell getting him to sleep."

Jeanette shrugged, "Sometimes he's like that."

"Did you have fun?"

"I did. It was invigorating to be around artists again."

"You're always around artists."

"You mean your friends? It's not quite the same."

"You mean, it's a different medium."

"No," she corrected, "I mean being seen as an equal."

He went silent, didn't correct her.

"I don't fit in with your set because I don't want to talk about Proust until my tongue falls out and, while I have read *Swann's Way*, I don't *feel* it the way I feel paintings. I understand swirls of color becoming something whole. I don't want to dissect every word of the novel, I want to breathe them, like art. It's different."

Oliver rose from the chair, "I'm going to bed. It's been a stressful evening."

She resisted rolling her eyes and bid him goodnight.

Jeanette wasn't sure when they had become roommates rather than lovers, parents, friends, she felt them drifting away from one another like polarized magnets. Trying to strain against the change, she suspected, would be futile. And yet, it made her sad. He had loved her, she knew this to be true, but perhaps love didn't last in the wake of reality and responsibilities. Maybe that was the secret of every modern relationship: there was no such thing as love.

She filled up a cup with water, washed her face, joined him in bed, woke in the night when Albert cried.

This was her life built on choices she had supported. Wasn't it?

Over the next few months, Jeanette threw herself into painting, and convincing Albert to begin trying solid food. He was less petulant and more content now, he would keep himself entertained inside his playpen with various toys while Jeanette worked on her dark still life paintings. They'd grown even larger now, one took up most of their bedroom wall. Oliver responded by spending less and less time with her, coming in the bedroom only to grab clothing and retreat once more.

Albie cried and Jeanette would rock his swing with her foot while she gessoed canvas. His cries became more foreign, farther away as the muse would take her down an unrelated path. Suddenly, she would be absorbed by something other than reality and the baby seemed an alien thing, disconnected from her.

Each day, the paintings closed in around her more tightly, leaning overhead like pressing shadows, blotting out the sun. In the evenings, she washed her brushes with turpentine and let the smell linger on her hands, her clothes, pretending that she lived inside one of her creations instead.

Albie crawled through her piles of paintings like an earthworm, flesh-toned, burrowing into the earth, shitting out of both ends. The stench brought her back to reality.

Eventually, the coffeehouse sold her second painting and requested more for the next show. She gave them two more, and was subsequently contacted by a small gallery who also hung one of her dead flower arrangements in the window. In this one, she used the same red throw as an accent, a different assortment of dried and drooping plants, and the addition of natural elements: a rock, a small bird's skull. The paintings had a layered, mostly black background that revealed occasional stripes of color, red, violet, from her initial layering, black always being the final layer. Jeanette's thematic oeuvre set itself upon each canvas and she painted with increased confidence.

Meanwhile, the latest issue of *Parabolas* was going through its final editing stages. Oliver had put in one of his own written pieces and a co-editor, Travis, had complained of bias. Oliver was worried the magazine was falling apart, but he also desperately wanted his own piece to appear on the website. They had talked about the issue for a week or so, Jeanette firmly taking Oliver's side whenever he mentioned the matter. Personally, she thought the entire thing smacked of vanity, particularly when they only had a couple hundred website visitors a month. After all, who cared if he inserted a little of his own writing into it? The hypotheticals had made them close again and they'd made love several times in the intervening days.

Oliver arrived home one day, after teaching. He had a quizzical expression on his face, Jeanette sensed a conversation brewing. She went to make some herbal tea.

"Have you been selling your paintings?" he asked.

Oh, it was about this, she realized.

"Yes. Why?"

"I thought I saw one of them hanging in the gallery downtown."

"You probably did."

"Why didn't you tell me?"

"Well, you've been so busy. And you didn't seem to appreciate my taking over the walls with paintings, so I didn't mention it. I just wanted to do something for myself."

"Is that what you've been doing when the nanny is here?"

"Yes."

"So, I've been wasting money on babysitting while you're out there peddling your wares to the highest bidder."

"You mean Adele's money, and that's hardly what's happening. I just did a small show, my paintings sold, and there was a bit of interest in my work."

"A creative genius," he snarked.

"Hardly. I'm just a hard worker."

"Are you implying that I'm not?"

"No."

"And your work is on my dime."

"Adele's."

The kettle whistled and she poured water over two sachets of chamomile tea, she handed one mug to him and blew gently on her own. Usually, this gesture symbolized a ceasefire, a domestic ritual bringing them back to their reality.

Oliver took his mug, walked to the sink, poured the tea down the drain. He walked back out the door and into the empty evening.

Jeanette drank her tea alone at the table.

That night, Jeanette slept, spread out alone in the king-sized bed, and dreamed of the ocean. It looked exactly the same as it had the day that Oliver had taken her to their beach house, the sun melted into the horizon like an egg yolk. Jeanette stood in the water, waves lapping hungrily at her knees, the sand sucking her toes down, down. A sense of peacefulness spread over her.

Then, she heard the screaming, it was coming from the shore. Someone was screaming and pointing, out in the distance Jeanette saw the bobbing head of Albert, he wasn't moving, just floating there like a buoy. She began to swim toward him, already fearing the worst, that he'd followed her out there and drowned. She swam and swam but her body moved so slowly through the otherwise calm water.

When she reached the bobbing child's head, it was in fact a buoy, lurid and red and inhuman.

Jeanette looked back to shore and saw Adele standing near the ocean's edge, holding a damp Albert, wrapped in a towel, and smiling at her.

A wave overtook her head and she found herself underwater. It was cool and quiet and peaceful, but, again, swimming so slowly, she couldn't break the surface. She struggled, in vain, until everything went dark.

She woke up covered in sweat, gasping for air.

Their nanny didn't show up the next week, or the following. Oliver didn't address it and Jeanette didn't ask. She knew he'd simply told Adele to cancel it. He didn't fire Veronika, but she came only on Mondays and was asked not to do any laundry.

Jeanette refused to do dishes or laundry, in protest, and continued to paint, only now leaving her dirty underwear purposefully on the bathroom floor until she built a small pile and Oliver found it necessary to move it to the hamper.

Albert began to mobilize, crawling, trying to stand. Jeanette wanted to encourage him, but at the same time, she desperately wished he would simply stop so she could ready a few new pieces for a show. He touched things with his sticky, wet child fingers and, in her panic to keep his curiosity contained, she put a plastic gate in the hallway, separating him from her workspace. At first, he cried. Then, distracted by a stuffed rabbit, he became impassive once more.

Jeanette's new works were all based around found objects: the bird skull, revisited, detritus from the interior flap of a book, bookmark, plane ticket, receipt, roses she'd picked from the neighbor's garden. The paintings were all small 10"x10" and grouped together in a square comprised of four rows of four canvases. The effect was quite striking and required the viewer to lean in for a closer look.

She called it: "Stolen Moments."

Oliver never said anything, but Jeanette intuited that he'd lost his co-editor in the publishing disagreement. The next issue ran without his byline and Oliver, no longer a co-editor, assumed the full role of editor-in-chief.

One evening, knowing he had made plans to stay home, Jeanette blithely walked out the door in a new pair of high heels she'd bought at the thrift store, they were leather, the nicest things she'd ever owned, and still only twenty dollars. The money from her paintings she had used to reinvigorate her mostly dormant checking account. It felt good to have something of her own again.

"Where are you going?" Oliver demanded, watching her gather her purse and a light coat.

"To my art show."

"Art show? Where?"

"Yes, I have an art show this evening. It's at a new place," she left off the name, not wanting to risk him creating a scene, "But it shouldn't be a problem because you can watch Albert."

"I have plans, actually."

"Oh, well, you'll have to organize some babysitting then. Wish me luck," she trilled before walking out the door.

Jeanette didn't give the apartment a backwards thought as she plowed forward into the night. This was her first gallery show, with only a couple of other creators. She felt like a real artist, not just a window treatment for passersby, though that painting had sold last week as well. It had also sparked her to update her resume with recent shows and past publications.

The gallery was on a main strip, flanked by bars and trendy restaurants, mostly tapas and sushi. She picked up a pamphlet as soon as she'd walked in. Her face, in black and white, announced the motif of her "Stolen Moments" pieces and her education. She shamelessly claimed an MA in Art History.

"J, darling! You made it," the gallery assistant rushed toward her as soon as she hit the track lighting.

"Of course."

"Let me introduce you around..."

What ensued was an endless profusion of hand shaking with other gallery owners, artists, investors. She soaked in the admiration they lavished on her.

"Really dark, but in a good way."

"When are you coming to the East Coast? I have this little gallery..."

"Nice to meet you, let's connect later via email."

It turned out, the gallery made up for its small space in outsized trendiness. The other two artists, a glass work sculptor and an installation creator, both received the same attention. It seemed, that night, that they had all been chosen to sit upon the dais of success.

For Jeanette, she felt it was about time.

At the evening's end, her purse was laden with business cards, several copies of the pamphlet, and a couple of hunks of cheddar cheese from the buffet table.

Bjorn, the installation artist, asked if she'd like to come out for a drink. "Cecile and I just want to celebrate the evening." Cecile, it turned out, was the glass sculptor. She hadn't said a word all night and looked exceedingly uncomfortable. Jeanette spotted her smoking a little ways off from the gallery and smiled in recognition of a kindred spirit.

"Sure, that would be nice," she agreed.

The bar Bjorn chose was dark and smoky, a little French, Jeanette imagined Oliver might like it, then dismissed the thought. They ordered Old Fashioneds and toasted to their mutual success.

"I used to be a contractor," Bjorn explained, "I built things to other people's specifications all day and I just got sick of it. So, I sold my house and moved into a studio I found out about from some art friends, I just started building until someone noticed."

"I took a glass blowing class and my professor pushed me to do something new, 'not water pipes' he said. I thought he was joking, but I guess that's what most of it really is. Anyway, I started making vaginas and I think he thought that was only moderately better, but here I am," Cecile chuckled a little. Her voice was quiet and hoarse, as though she'd already worn herself out talking to someone else.

"I started painting to understand myself again," Jeanette offered. "Then I wanted to share what I'd learned with someone else."

Cecile nodded, "Exactly."

"We create art because we have too much inside," Bjorn agreed.

They toasted once more and began to discuss the show itself.

"A nice gallery..."

"The owner had a very odd toupee."

"Was that a toupee? I feel so misled!"

They ordered a second round and began to laugh about their undergrad years, the outsized egos of people in their programs, certain they would be Andy Warhol's second coming.

"I was in a class with this guy who kept going on and on about a literary magazine he wanted to create," Cecile laughed. "He wanted to put it online to democratize art, but you could tell, it was really only to publish his own friends and soothe all of their fragile egos."

Jeanette didn't have to ask who the undergrad was, their college wasn't that big.

It wasn't late when she left the bar, but she felt a thousand years older than when she'd entered. The street still surged with couples on dates, groups of friends leaving the bars, people heading to a second, or third, destination. She joined the throng and was pushed along by their movement, heedless of her surroundings.

She paused to find a cigarette and peered into one of the shiny, modern spaces that lined the street. At the bar she saw someone who looked like Oliver, almost an exact twin. She laughed to herself, it was a proven brain trick that strangers sometimes resembled a person who often occupied your own personal thoughts. He was a doppelgänger. She tilted her head to light the cigarette and noticed a woman joining him. Perhaps my own doppelgänger, Jeanette laughed.

But it wasn't.

This woman was younger, blonde. She looked somehow familiar to Jeanette as well. Despite the whiskey, Jeanette was quickly able to place her, Sofi Tremmel of the melancholic love poems. The concept of doubling disappeared as Jeanette realized Sofi was Oliver's plan that evening. They had martinis and Sofi put her hand companionably on Oliver's thigh. They kissed, it was tender in the way that lovers are, not in a sense of a passionate hookup, anyone could see this was an established relationship.

Jeanette began to cough, sputtering, reaching out blindly for something to steady her, and eventually finding a lamppost.

They hadn't seen her, she was certain, though she started walking and didn't look back until she reached the interior of the apartment where a woman she didn't know was sitting on their couch.

"Hello, I'm Laura. Oliver told me to expect you a little later."

"How much do I owe you?" Jeanette whispered, her voice ragged sounding.

"Oh, Oliver already paid me..."

"Then could you please leave."

The woman hurriedly collected her belongings and exited the apartment. Jeanette collapsed, replacing her on the couch. The leather pumps she'd felt so proud of had rubbed angry blisters on the backs of her ankles.

Of course he'd found someone else, and of course she was younger and literary, Jeanette chided herself.

The rush of excitement, success, companionship she'd felt

earlier in the evening dissipated entirely. She went in to check on Albert, he was fast asleep, then ran herself a bath, drank half a bottle of white wine and, when Oliver still had not returned home, she passed out in her own version of a coma.

The phone rang early, too early, light had not yet reached the color of pink grapefruits and Oliver was not beside her in bed. The ringing brought consciousness back into her body, her head pounded and her mouth was fuzzy with sleep. Nude under her bathrobe that she'd neglected to change out of the night before, she staggered to the phone, hoping Albert had not yet woken.

"Hello?" Her voice was bleary around the edges, clearly freshly aware of the world.

"I'm so sorry, hun. Did I wake you?" Marian's girlish chuckle rubbed Jeanette the exact wrong way.

"To be honest, yes."

"Sorry sorry. I was wondering if Ollie was still planning to come to LA next week?"

"I wouldn't know."

"What do you mean?"

"I'm not his personal assistant. I don't know what his plans are. I couldn't possibly."

Marian paused, "He didn't tell you he was coming to see me?"

"He did not."

"I thought, well, the room is reserved for two..."

Jeanette barked a harsh laugh filled with broken glass and rage.

"Yes, I'm sure it is. Only the second person isn't me."

She placed the phone back on the receiver. Albert had started to whine and she covered her ears in protest. Everything was too loud all of a sudden. She got back in bed and pulled the covers over her, blotting out the sun, the phone, the whines of her child.

Marian didn't call back and Oliver finally returned midday, by which point Jeanette had bathed both herself and Albert. She'd situated the child in his high chair and was letting him play with Cherrios while she painted. She didn't look up when Oliver entered, though she could smell him from across the room. He hadn't showered.

"You know, darling, we haven't even planned a first birthday for Albert," Jeanette noted.

"No," he answered. "We haven't."

"Well, why don't you ask your mother if she'd be interested in helping out. Oh, and call Marian back, she wanted to check with us about our hotel for LA. I had no idea you were planning to take me on a trip, what a surprise."

"What? No. That was a work trip, I was just going to pop in and see her."

"I'd love to go and do a little shopping around the galleries there, maybe bring some of my prints. It would be a good opportunity." She lavished a last bit of paint onto a blood red rose, then announced, "But first, the party!"

They set a date for three weeks out. Thus, with the party concept in full swing and Adele amply involved, Jeanette was able to regain use of their nanny one or two days a week. Oliver tried to avoid any interaction and would only 'yes' or 'no' balloon types under extreme duress, mostly he absented himself. LA was not mentioned again, by anyone.

Her days were filled with streamers, testing sparkling wines with Adele, and organizing a caterer. Naturally, Adele thought the party should be for adults, the baby was merely being a prop to show off. It didn't matter. Jeanette used all of her free time to paint and write. During the third week, she left the apartment with an armload of paintings and a mind full of wandering thoughts, she'd been alone and brooding for too long and it had become something else. First, she dropped the larger part of the bundle off at her gallery, she had begun to consider it 'hers,' and had a fairly lengthy chat with the curator. They shook hands and she proceeded onward. A single piece Jeanette kept under her arm as she walked through the park, back to 'her' side of town.

Vihaan was, as ever, ensconced in his store.

"I brought you something," Jeanette greeted him.

He turned his head to look at her.

"It's you!"

"Of course it's me. Now, here." She lay one of her small, found object paintings in front of him. It was of the Indian milk candy he'd given her so long ago. She'd taken a photograph, then painted it. "This is my thank you."

"For what?" he asked, his eyebrows raised in surprise.

"For being my friend."

He smiled at her, showing all his teeth. "This is beautiful. Thank you."

To show his immediate appreciation, he took a thumbtack and shoved it into the wall, then hung the canvas there, just behind his shoulder, visible to anyone who came into the store.

"See? Now I can show people I know a famous artist and she likes Indian candy."

They both laughed, then settled in to watch part of a Bollywood tape together. Vihaan tried to show her the dance, but they kept laughing more and more, never quite getting past the first two hand motions. When the movie ended, he sent her back out with a cup of his chai tea.

It braced her for her final errand.

Back at the apartment, Adele and Oliver were playing with Albert on the floor. He was cooing and laughing. Jeanette paused for a moment to watch. They looked like one of the families from the park, a Norman Rockwell painting, finally, with none of the darker undertones. It was all bright highlights, smiles, and chubby, healthy babies. As she stepped into the frame, their faces fell. Adele picked up Albert and held him to her chest, using his hunger as an excuse to go to the kitchen. Oliver sat back on the couch, embarrassed to have been caught in an act of joy. The painting, now a mosaic, broken at the edges.

"Hello," she said.

He nodded.

"I was dropping some paintings off at the gallery."

"I figured."

"The party's a go for this weekend?"

"Yes."

"Good."

He rose to leave, to shutter himself in the study for the rest of the evening.

"Wait," Jeanette said. What came next could have been anything, or everything, but what she actually said was, "I need you to sign a few things for the party rentals."

He sighed, taking her proffered pen and neatly affixing his name to two pages, without reading them, as she suspected he would. Not reading something was his form of the deepest insult. He handed her back the pen and offered her an expression that said simply, 'Are we done now?'

"Yes, that's all. Thank you, Oliver."

He shut the door to his office, she heard a book fall to the floor with a heavy thud, an appropriate punctuation, and placed the papers inside her painting supplies.

Jeanette spent the night before the party staring at her laptop until her eyes crossed. It was plain to her now that Sofi Tremmel's tragic love poems were all directed at Oliver, including the most recent ones. His story, the one he'd pushed so hard to have published, was the response. It was about a honeymoon in Cuba: two couples go on a trip together, they both end up fighting and the wronged husband from the first pair finds the wronged wife from the second, creating the more significant couple from the broken pieces of their past. It was soppy, written with a Hemingway abruptness, even down to the Cuban obsession, that Jeanette considered to be beneath Oliver. He'd hurt her, but he wasn't a hack. The truth was, *Parabolas* had simply been the stage upon which they could act out their nascent love affair.

The good Scotch was in the top cabinet in their kitchen. Jeanette dragged a chair across the dining room floor and reached for the bottle, pouring a couple of fingers over ice. She cracked her knuckles, then began to write. It was well after two in the morning when she joined Oliver in bed. His eyes looked more creased than she remembered, even in sleep. His face was relaxed, kind. She remembered that face and stroked it gently.

"I loved you," she whispered into his freshly shampooed hair. It was easier to say now.

When the morning came, they found themselves tangled together in the sheets. Their bodies had sought to conjoin in the dreamworld. Oliver quickly extricated himself, cleared his throat, and made for the bathroom. Although not before Jeanette saw the telltale bulge in his boxer shorts.

"Too bad," she murmured, before rolling over to sleep for a few minutes more. Soon her apartment would be filled with strangers and salmon puffs, whatever those were. She spread her legs out horizontally across the bed, savoring every inch, every cool spot.

Oliver turned on the shower and Jeanette lay there listening to the sounds of people living, her own breath, the swishing sounds of her baby on the monitor. He'd be awake soon too, she'd feed him plums from a jar. She didn't have much time.

When Adele rang the doorbell, Jeanette was ready. Albert was wearing a bow tie with his posh baby suit, it was already covered in plum drool, but that hardly mattered. Adele swept him up in her arms and began to coo. She didn't acknowledge Jeanette, who shut the door behind her and returned to the kitchen where the caterers had dropped off the food. She arranged each group of canapés artfully on wide, white plates, little sprigs of herbs around the edges.

Adele took over opening the door and welcoming the guests were were most definitely hers. They passed by Jeanette as though she were the silent help in the background. Everyone oo-ed and ahh-ed over baby Albert, passed him around from arm to arm.

A few of Oliver's friends, she recognized them from the parties she had attended a lifetime ago, entered and, amazingly, Sofi Tremmel along with them. To her credit, she looked incredibly uncomfortable. Jeanette stepped back into the kitchen a little further to watch her marvel at Oliver's secret life, the one Sofi had, no doubt, been trying to plumb for months. Now she'd made it, she had penetrated the wall to his innermost fortress.

Jeanette wiped her hands on a kitchen towel, picked up a glass of champagne and approached the group.

"So glad you made it," she called, a little too loudly.

Their eyes all darted to her, took her in. She knew she looked good. Her hair was curled, she wore a black turtleneck and black pedal pushers with ballet flats, red lipstick and a little mascara. She preened a little under their gaze.

"Come in, we have champagne, snacks, and of course, a baby."

Sofi tried to edge past her, her eyes focused on the ground.

"We haven't met," Jeanette smiled at her, extending her hand. "I'm Jeanette."

"Sofi," the girl whispered.

"A pleasure. Make yourself at home, I'm sure you'll have no trouble."

Sofi stood, anchored to the same spot, and Jeanette returned to her canapés arranging, which is where Marian eventually found her.

"Jeanette."

She was on her second glass of champagne and not in the mood.

"Hello Marian."

"I just wanted to say... well, Thomas is here too."

"I assumed."

"I'm really sorry about the LA trip. I didn't know you were having any trouble with Ollie."

Jeanette interrupted her, "If you'd like to meet trouble, she's the blonde one over there. Now, please let me finish this last plate."

Later, she saw Marian quietly berating Oliver in a corner. He looked appropriately chastened, but Sofi was now holding court with the young men of Oliver's friend group, they were all vying for her attention. Despite Marian's admonition, Oliver pushed himself into their center, to place himself at Sofi's side. She looked relieved and pleased he had so obviously claimed her.

Albert had passed out in his playpen from overstimulation at this point. Jeanette approached him and kissed his soft baby down forehead. She closed her eyes and tried to force her body to feel a profound sensation of love, pride, loss, but she felt nothing, a duty-bound spider carrying the burden of her eggs. Albert rolled onto his side and slept on.

It was her cue.

PART THREE

Later, they'd all wonder when was the last time they saw her.

Was it by the canapés? Or when she put Albert down for a nap in his crib? Had they seen her at all?

Certainly, Oliver knew where she'd gone. The guests, seeking to leave, to say their goodbyes, went to question him regarding the whereabouts of the mother. He was crowded on the fire escape with his friends, chatting, smoking.

"Mum's inside," he explained, turning away from them.

"Not your mother, the mother of your child."

Jeanette crossed his mind for the first time in what seemed like hours. The party had proceeded swimmingly, much thanks to Adele's careful planning. Everyone stayed late, drank heartily, and complimented the food, which she, of course, took credit for despite everyone knowing it was all catered. The birthday boy smashed a quiche into his mouth and clapped at the toys people laid at his princely feet. Oliver had tried to forget about the morning, his body, confused by the warmth of her legs, the sleepy invitation of her caress. In response, he opened their good Scotch and found it lighter than he remembered, shared the rest with his friends, with Sofi, even though she hated Scotch. She took small sips with a displeased pucker. They were all pleasantly tipsy when the partygoers came looking.

"Well?" they were growing impatient.

"I'm not sure. Check Albert's room."

"We did."

"The kitchen?"

"No one there."

"She probably stepped out for a smoke. Don't worry, I'll tell her you had a great time."

Marian popped her head out next, "We're leaving Ollie." She made pointed eye contact with only him.

He kissed her cheek dismissively. Thomas waved from inside, not wishing to risk Marian's ire in speaking with him. He waved back.

Marian, he should be mad at her, not the other way around. She'd somehow let slip that he was planning a getaway with Sofi. Of course, he'd meant to see her there, to explain the situation calmly and let Sofi charm her the way Jeanette had.

"Jeanette is difficult, prickly, distant," he tried to explain.

"That's what you said you loved about her," Marian protested. "You can't expect a person to change who they are via your silent telepathy, Ollie. Let me guess, this new girl is 'sweet' and 'easy.'"

"She's smart too, a good writer, really creative. You've got to read some of her poetry," he knew he was piling it on, but couldn't stop himself. She had put him on the defensive.

"You don't think Jeanette is creative?"

Oliver didn't respond. Of course he thought she was bloody creative, but she'd turned their entire apartment into her personal studio and there was no place for him among her and the paintings and the baby. She'd made her intangible obsession with art a very tangible inconvenience for him. And, besides, what about his own creative endeavors, where was the space for that amid her profusion of talent and growing success? Was he just supposed to be a part-time professor with his daddy's trust fund for the rest of his life?

"That's not the point," he finally argued, too late now.

Marian leaned toward him, angrily whispered over the din of

the party, "Ollie, you're an idiot. Worse than that, you're a fucking cliche." Her breath left a warm sensation on his neck like a brand.

She hadn't spoken to him again until they'd bid farewell through the window.

Had she sought out Jeanette, said something cruel to her, he suddenly wondered. Maybe that's why she'd run off. More likely, the party was just too much for her, he acknowledged. She wasn't much on people, particularly Adele's people, and he had to admit she had been trying the past few weeks to make everything run smoothly. Though somehow the party felt like a form of punishment for his behavior the night of her gallery show.

She wasn't cruel toward Albert, despite having a hard time at first. He'd heard her crying, an endless weeping that went on for nights. One night, she'd whispered in his ear, 'Was it a mistake?' and he'd assured her, 'No, no no,' until she fell back asleep. And here he was, drunk on the fire escape, at his son's birthday party, and she had absented herself. He could have said, 'maybe,' but what good would that have done anyone?

Sofi looked up at him now with glassy eyes. She'd had too much to drink. His friends were loudly discussing Confucianism and Oliver wanted to shout, "Just shut up!" He needed a coffee.

"Alright, time to go boys," he announced, playacting the carefree bachelor he once was. He wrapped his arms casually around their shoulders as they flicked their cigarettes over the railing and into the night, orange sparks on the sidewalk below.

Inside, Adele put her finger to her lips and they all tiptoed past the sleeping princeling like naughty schoolchildren. A few hangers-on assisted Adele in the clean up and Oliver walked his friends to the door, resisting the urge to shove them more quickly away.

Sofi opened her mouth, closed it, opened it again. She resembled a confused goldfish and Oliver suddenly felt an overwhelming rush of tenderness and pity towards her, the poor, helpless thing. In a surge of emotion, he leaned forward and embraced her, too tightly, whispered into her hair, "I'll call you tonight." Her eyes smiled as she was pulled away, someone called out, "Rob's got a cab!" and everyone beat a hasty retreat downstairs.

Adele stood, clutching a plastic bag of garbage and watching from the living room.

◇

The thing with Sofi hadn't been intentional. He hadn't been actively seeking someone else. Marian just needed to hear the entire story before she went around making assumptions, but she hadn't given him a chance to speak, to explain.

The day was warm, like most days here, and Oliver had just finished teaching three classes in a row. The thrall of his 101 course students thrilled him one minute and frustrated him the next. He sat at his desk, tapping his pencil, and attempting to form a lecture that bridged the gap between Shakespeare and Grendel without asking for too much in terms of written work. He still had a stack of papers to grade from two weeks prior staring accusingly at him.

He shared his office with another adjunct, a small closet at the end of the English department's looming hallway that barely accommodated a pair of desks and chairs. All day he graded papers, back to back with his colleague who brought in sauerkraut and sausage sandwiches from the deli that stank even after the trash had been taken out. Their small, square window didn't open so the air simply loomed with rotten cabbage. Sofi came to the door that day, knocked once, then stuck her head in. She wore a diaphanous red dress with spaghetti straps and brought with her a trail of sunshine, something fresh and springlike, in her wake. He sniffed the air.

"Excuse me, are you Professor Leroy?"

"I am," Oliver confirmed. He pushed his chair back to accommodate her in the space and only served to jam his hand between both chairs, resulting in a sharp pain. He clenched his jaw in what he hoped was a masculine denial of injury and smiled at her.

"You run the *Parabolas* magazine, right?"

"I do. How did you hear about it?"

"Someone posted about it on the student forum."

"I see." He was slightly taken aback by the quick awareness and connectedness brought about by the Internet.

"Well, I have some poems..." she continued. Her arms were outstretched toward him, trembling, making the papers she held shiver in the air.

She was earnest, so open, about her tender, unformed words. He had fought with Jeanette that morning and her dark, brooding paintings, her black outfits, they existed in stark contrast to Sofi's soft loveliness. The grass is always greener and all that, he acknowledged.

Still, he took the poems, said he would read them, told her to come back tomorrow. He prioritized her over his own students without a backward thought, shoving them in his bag before heading home.

The apartment was quiet and dark, Albert was playing in his play pen, Jeanette was in the bedroom painting something huge and obscure, she had created another living golem that sucked all life from the room. He took one look at the layered colors, the broad streaks of black, harsh and bleak across the canvas. He decided immediately that he hated it.

"Did you make dinner?" Oliver asked.

"Does it look like I made dinner?" she retorted.

He felt as if he'd asked her to walk barefoot over glass. Was it really that much to make him a hot meal? Couldn't she just pretend she was making it only for herself and save him a bit? Uninterested in another argument, he sighed and went to the fridge he knew was empty, just to look, then ordered Pad Thai.

Jeanette put Albert to bed in the crib, then emerged from their bedroom, paint-smeared, her hair pinned up in a messy bun, day old eyeliner around her eyes. She looked beautiful. Oliver couldn't help but smile at her. She smiled back.

"What's up?"

"I ordered Thai."

"You read my mind."

She went to the window to smoke a cigarette on the fire escape.

"It's warm. Come outside with me?" She held out her hand, her fingertips red and purple from moving paint around, in the low light they looked like a bruise, or the plague.

He followed her.

They sat together in the balmy night, toes almost, but not quite, touching, passing a cigarette back and forth, pretending they were simple people with simple wants when really they both wanted to own the moon.

In the morning, the sun gazed through the window of Oliver's home office, his respite from the real world. Jeanette called it his 'Fortress of Solitude,' and he didn't dispute her. It was here, without the intrusions of harried students and fellow professors, without the pervasive cabbage smell, he was able to get real work done. On each wall were bookshelves, well-stocked with classic fiction and nonfiction books about interesting topics like summiting Mount Everest. His desk sat under the window, facing out, so he could view the trees that reached up toward their building. It made him feel as though he were writing in a treehouse.

Extracting his red writing notebook, Oliver realized he'd forgotten all about Sofi's poems. They fluttered to the ground in a sad little heap and he hurled himself forward to collect them from that state.

Each poem was melancholic, nostalgic, the memories of being a girl, catching fireflies, red lipstick on a boy's cheek. Then there was one, a particular one, about a dapper man in a tailored blazer, plaid with elbow patches, and alarmingly like his own. He was married and smart and distracted, would he ever notice her? In the end, he does not, but the poem's narrator pines for him from afar.

Naturally, Oliver inserted himself into the narrative.

As a joke, he decided to write his own flash fiction piece in the form of a response. Just five hundred words of a sad man, locked away from the interesting world and invested in the drudgery of family life. He wished for a nymph, a muse, to come to him and free his creative mind from his woeful, world-bound body. Eventually, one of the Greek muses offers her services in exchange for his earthly voice. He would never run out of things to write, but he would never speak again, silently longing for that which he could never possess. In his story, when the muse appeared, she wore a flowing red gown.

Trite, he admonished himself.

Together, though, the pair told a cohesive story that he enjoyed. He read them, alternating their order, connecting the ideas to one another like blood vessels, creating a the feeling of lust, of longing. He felt himself growing hard as he read it for the third time.

Sofi came to his office that afternoon, as she said she would, her face expectant.

"These are..." he paused. "Really emotive."

She immediately blushed.

"I think you have some real potential."

"You do?"

"Sure. I want to publish one in this issue and maybe a second one in the following issue, this one, about the professor."

Her neck reddened further and he pretended not to notice.

"There's an attention to detail that I really like."

He handed the rest back to her and she looked at him, pink and exultant, filled with validation.

"Would you like to get a coffee?" he asked. "We can talk some more about poetry, writing."

"Yes, definitely."

By the end of their coffee date, she had agreed to work as an intern for *Parabolas*, though Oliver didn't quite remember his reasoning behind asking her.

Later that night, he imagined himself on a faraway tropical island. Somewhere warm and tropical. He wrote about two couples, unhappy, and how the disparate pieces of each pairing found their way together. The professor falls in love with his best friend's wife, they are the chosen ones. The ones meant to be together. It was a more cohesive story than his first attempt, he titled it 'The Lost Honeymoon.'

He wondered later if what Marian had called him, a cliche, wasn't in fact completely accurate.

One summer afternoon, after making love countless times, Jeanette swung her bare leg over his and, while lighting a cigarette that they shared on her futon mattress, she recounted for him the story of her advising grad professor almost hitting on her.

"I could tell he wanted to, that he almost did it. I wanted to dare him to, ask him if I was worth it, but I didn't. And he's never made me sit with him in that stuffy office again. I deem it a victory for womankind."

She passed him the cigarette. He always worried that she'd lose interest halfway through and burn him, either by design or by accident.

But Sofi wasn't his student any more than Jeanette had been. She was a student who happened to attend the university, who was majoring in French, and who wrote poems on the back of paper bar napkins. He'd watched her do it, fascinated by the brazenness of it, pouring her raw emotions out in the middle of a bar.

Objectively, her poetry was not good. Oliver had tried to reconcile the fact that earnestness did not beget talent, and yet he'd published them. Of course he had, he admired her in the same way he had once admired Jeanette. He wanted to give her a chance.

However, when he submitted the second poem, and his own piece, his co-editor, Travis, had balked at the idea.

"These are just so..."

"Emotive?"

"Smarmy."

"What?"

"I don't want to publish some crappy poetry that got your dick hard, I want to publish things that are challenging convention, creating revolution. This is just sappy Edwardian shit."

"And as co-editor, I feel our magazine could use some diversity."

"Diversity, sure. But this muddies the tone, it undermines what we actually claim to want!"

"It shows open-mindedness."

"It shows a lack of quality control."

They'd argued, intensely, for a while before Travis, in the heat of the moment, left *Parabolas* with both his potential and his html skills. Oliver considered going after him, but his pride prevented it.

That night, he complained to Jeanette, artfully omitting the fact that his piece was essentially a companion to Sofi's. Not that it mattered, she didn't know Sofi, didn't pay attention to who he'd taken on as an intern, now that she was no longer on campus.

"Travis accused me of bias for wanting to insert my own writing into the magazine."

"Did you put anything of yours in the debut issue?"

"No, of course not."

"Well, I don't know what he'd be complaining about then. It's your creation, who cares if you put a little of yourself into it?"

He could tell she was holding back, but he appreciated her support.

Later, he lamented, "I am worried the magazine is crumbling."

"That's slightly melodramatic."

"It *is* my creation though, my child."

"You have a real child."

He conceded her point and let it drop, pressing publish on their third issue and sending it out into the world one week later.

Of course Sofi read his story. Hadn't he planned for her to?

She appeared in his office doorway like an apparition.

"Did you write it for me?" she asked, directly.

"Yes," he answered.

Her eyes widened and she crossed the small room in two steps to kiss him, her soft lips slightly parted, met his own. He kissed her back, allowing the moment to linger. And that's what started it.

Oliver wanted to imagine he'd seduced her with his prose, but perhaps he'd only seduced her by feeding her her own vision of herself, by giving her a mirror, the thing all women truly craved. He had started to doubt everything.

"Albert is asleep, he had a big day," Adele told him, startling Oliver out of his kitchen reverie. He stood over the sink, holding a glass filled with only the barest remnants of Scotch. The apartment was otherwise empty.

"Yes. It was lovely mum, thank you."

A pause. He knew she was going to ask.

"Do you know where she went?"

"I don't."

"Can you call her friends?"

"I don't know any of her friends. I don't know if she even has any friends," he admitted in a sigh.

"Ollie, you must have some idea."

"No, mum. I have no idea. We had very separate social lives lately."

Adele was quiet. "I'm going to take the trash down."

He didn't protest, just stared at the Scotch glass. It was one of Jeanette's earlier acquisitions, an ostentatious cut crystal piece that matched nothing else in their cupboard and probably cost her something like fifty cents. Everything she collected was that way, mismatched, one of a kind, an absolute steal, unbearably ugly.

When Oliver had first seen her apartment, that rat hole on the far side of town where she'd slept on the floor and grown stolen plants, the austere but aesthetically curated nature of it struck him. At first glance, he felt like he'd walked into a hippie garage sale. No one he knew would be unselfconscious enough to live in such a haphazard way. Somehow Jeanette made it beautiful, kicked off her sandals and began to dance to a jazz record. Her comfort disarmed him. She sensed his latent snobbishness immediately, flushed out the aspect of himself he most often tried to hide, and rejected him for it.

In recompense, he'd had no choice but to expose his own embarrassing pieces to receive her forgiveness. Yes, he was rich, he owned matching plates, he had an apartment with an extra room he never used, they owned a beach house, his mother was French and wore designer clothes and organized children's parties to have salmon croquettes and zero children. His own literary magazine editor pretensions were largely an outsized attempt to make people forget about this fact, or pretend not to notice it.

Still, how was he any different than any other writer who originally came from a place of privilege to create something great? Was his art any less worthy?

Jeanette might have said yes, so he never asked her.

With Adele downstairs, he walked into the living room. It felt so empty, devoid of guests and noise, none of Jeanette's soft jazz records or the warmth of her presence. Everything felt unbalanced.

Oliver wandered into his office, pausing momentarily to listen for Albert, but there was no sound. The papers on his desk had been stacked and arranged, he doubted Jeanette had tidied, but momentarily panicked as to what she might have happened across. Of course there was nothing, he was careful. Just his credit card statement, but Jeanette had shown little interest in his finances or what he spent money on. She didn't pry.

Her aloofness had drawn him in, initially. The way she allowed him to have his own life and interests, yet still possess some small part of her. Albert, before he was Albert, was Oliver's key to possessing the rest. Or that had been the plan.

He still couldn't believe she'd left the party so abruptly, her own son's party. He suspected she had some art deal, maybe even a show, and considered it his repayment for the afternoons she'd spent with Adele.

At the center of the desk was something he didn't recognize, something written not in his own hand. Oliver's initial thought was that it was some ill-formed romantic idea of Sofi's to leave a poem on his desk, he cringed. But as he approached, he saw it was, in fact a picture, a note, set atop a packet of other printed pages.

The note, a sticky note written in Jeanette's tight handwriting, stated simply: *This is not my life. Goodbye. – J*

His breath caught. He peeled the sticky note from its resting place and held it closer, though further inspection brought nothing, no hidden message, no indentations or eraser marks of previous drafts. This simple, terse message extended Oliver's mind into all manner of imaginings, aside from the most obvious realization: she was gone.

This was, however, confirmed after he turned his attention to the photo. Cut like a picture from an old yearbook, the black and white square had the grainy quality of a cheap printer. Still, he recognized it immediately, it was a picture he had looked at often, the picture Sofi Tremmel had submitted to accompany her poems on the *Parabolas* website.

Oliver turned the square over, anticipating another note, but there was nothing.

His hands shook as he reached for the remaining packet of papers, hesitant of what unwelcome surprise might be contained within. His trepidation was not without merit.

The papers were legal documents, notarized, official-looking, and titled: 'Termination of Parental Rights.'

He skimmed the pages, but his eyes kept zooming in, then out, his neck awash in a prickling cold sweat. Nausea from the Scotch, the salmon, and all this — this betrayal, he wanted to cry out — threatened to overtake him. He gagged, bitter saliva filling his mouth.

Worst of all, his own signature, yes it was definitely his, was affixed to the bottom of the page.

He vaguely remembered rushing through the signing of some catering forms she'd thrust at him, her temperament mellowed. At the time, he had simply wanted to escape her, afraid she would sense Sofi on him, take Albert away. Would she even have cared? Had he ever mattered to her? In the end, he had signed the papers without reading them and disappeared into the office to stare at his bookshelf and pretend to grade student essays.

Despite his own mild efforts at escapism, somehow she had disappeared everything and vanished without making a sound.

Oliver realized he'd had a child with a ghost.

"What do you want to do with your life, you know, after graduation?" Oliver asked on one of the many afternoons they spent at Jeanette's apartment during that hazy summer.

It was so hot, everything felt as though it were on fire. Jeanette wore one of his button down shirts, buttoned only at her waist, and boy short underpants. He was wearing boxers, nothing else. They were crowded next to the window air conditioning unit that sometimes worked and sometimes shorted out, turning off all of the lights, until they could flip the breaker back on.

"I'm doing it," Jeanette replied.

"What do you mean?"

"I wanted to move here, have a couple of love affairs, then graduate."

"Don't you have any plans beyond the degree?"

"No. I don't make plans, they tend to not work out and then everyone's left disappointed. This is a fucking hot box, let's go get a pint of ice cream and try not to think too hard about anything. I'm afraid our brains will fry."

Oliver didn't press it. He thought of her as a free spirit, albeit directionless.

He thought she'd take to motherhood, that it would give her life purpose. He thought it was a path she could forge in her own way. And I suppose she did, he acknowledged.

Oliver explained the situation to Adele, omitting the photograph of Sofi, his own part in the betrayal. He sensed she had already made the connection, but wanted to avoid a dressing down.

"She has abandoned her family! What kind of mother would do that? What kind of a woman is she?" Adele raged in the living room.

"The kind that probably never wanted to be a mother to begin with," Oliver stated, still ready to defend her to his mother.

Her yelling woke Albert and Oliver rushed into the room to quiet him. He picked him up, brought him to the rocking chair and began the ceaseless, monotonous movement that babies enjoyed. The child calmed down almost immediately. Holding his son to his chest, his legs slowly moving forward, then back, Oliver felt tears prick his eyes. This was it now, the soft baby down head rested on his shoulders, burbled, then slept again.

Oliver replaced him into the crib and returned to a fuming Adele pacing circles in the living room.

"You're just going to have to get her back," she stage whispered at him.

"I told you, I don't know where she's gone..."

"We'll start with the airlines..."

"...and even if I did..."

"...then I will call the trains."

"...I wouldn't force her to come back."

Adele was no longer listening. She had the receiver in one hand, a phone book in the other, ready to do battle. His mother, ever ready to take control of the situation. She could have been an Army general. He remembered how she'd begged, pleaded with him to keep the baby, before he was Albert, when he was still a cluster of cells. "Oliver, you have to do the right thing," she'd insisted. What if the "right thing" wasn't the right thing, he'd wanted to ask, but didn't. Now, of course, he couldn't imagine Albie not existing. But then, he also couldn't imagine Jeanette being gone.

However, after several hours of calling and research and reheating of leftovers from the caterer, Adele came up empty-handed.

As Oliver could have told her, Jeanette wouldn't be on any flight manifests or train schedules. She would have had a better plan than that.

Defeated, Adele left him alone, with promises to return tomorrow, to report Jeanette as a missing person to the police. "They will have to do something," she insisted, before turning on her heel to leave the apartment.

Oliver did not relish the idea of police officers looking at their apartment, their inner life, his inability to answer any questions as to her whereabouts, the picture, the note. No, he decided, they would not call the police. He didn't have anyone to call at all. Most of his friends knew about Sofi and would be unsurprised, Marian would also take Jeanette's side, surely.

The cut crystal glass sat on the edge of the sink, its accusing glare glinting in his direction. He watched his arm angrily swat it into the sink where it shattered into tiny pieces, like ice.

A week passed, then two. Nothing came from Jeanette, no new clues.

This is not my life, played on repeat in Oliver's head.

He was now living the life she had fully participated in creating, he was raising a son whose first home had been inside her. Did she really feel this didn't belong to her?

Sofi called, he didn't answer.

Adele stopped by with food.

He attended his classes, gave stone-faced lectures, then returned to his empty apartment, his nanny, his child, and the collective concerned stares of anyone who came into contact with him. A thick veneer of self-pity emanated from deep within his bones.

"Is he eating?" Marian asked Adele over the phone.

"I think so."

"What about Albie?"

"He's fine, I saw him today. I went ahead and asked the nanny to come three days a week, I go by for a visit on the other days."

"And no word from Jeanette?"

"No," Adele spat. "Best case scenario, he won't even remember her."

Marian didn't ask which 'he' she was referring to.

Oliver found a pack of her cigarettes, discarded and tucked away under the bed. Although he'd found other remnants, bits of proof she'd been there, in the intervening weeks, there wasn't much. He held the crumpled pack in his hand. Two were missing, had been smoked, one had the telltale orange stain of her lipstick, as though she'd once considered lighting it, then changed her mind.

He walked to the fire escape, swung his legs out the window and straddled the ledge, a bit in both worlds. He dislodged a cigarette and smoked it slowly, recalling how he'd often find her sitting here, staring out at the darkness and thinking.

Was she thinking then about that other life? Her existence had always been in some ways intangible, like her feet never quite fully touched the ground.

Early on, when they spent their evenings in that pub near campus, a place he wouldn't have taken any other girl, but felt it would appeal to her, she sat across from him, peeling the label off a bottle of cheap beer.

"Where are you from?" he asked.

"Nowhere," she laughed.

"No one is from nowhere," he countered.

"Everywhere, then. But really a few towns, down South, and then out East, that don't warrant much of a mention."

Oliver was smoking and thinking about that conversation the day the first letter arrived.

Albert had begun walking, toddling a bit, then collapsing. His constant striving spurred Oliver onward as well and he'd poured himself back into his lectures, his classes. With this new walking development, though, came the inevitable discovery of new things, new places to reach, and Albert toddled toward him with a soggy envelope in his fist. He'd been chewing on the corner.

"Albie, no. Give that here," he pulled the envelope from his son's strong grip and replaced it with a stuffed animal. The child flopped to the floor happy to chew on that as a substitute.

The recipient name on the envelope was smudged: "Victoria J ...." but the address was his own.

He gripped the cigarette with his lips and turned his body fully inside the apartment. Who was 'Victoria'? Oliver had lived in the apartment for several years and, as far as he knew, the previous occupant was an elderly man. Still, hoping for a clue to Jeanette's whereabouts, he tore into the damp envelope.

The paper was thick and white and heavy in his hands, the writing, an endless cursive scrawl in something that resembled Sharpie marker.

"Dear V," it began.

He checked the envelope again, the return address was small, printed, and from a women's prison in Florida. The last name was the same as Jeanette's. He read on.

Dear V,

It was so good to git your last letter, thank you for the cash. They put it on my comissery account. And I know we ain't talked in a while, but things get so darn distracting here. The days git away from me. But I've been reading that book you sent, The Count of Monte Cristo, all about being locked up. I know how he feels. Anyway, I'm real proud of you bout the art stuff. Send me some more pictures soon.

Love you, Mom

Oliver read it twice. Then rose, picked up Albie who was still contentedly chewing on a stuffed elephant, walked into his office where the papers she'd signed were still sitting on the desk. He squinted at the signature, difficult to read in the waning evening light.

"Jeanette Victoria..."

He had never asked her middle name and, for some reason, this made him more ashamed than anything else he'd done.

Albie had fallen asleep by this point and Oliver laid him gently in the crib, his face slack with the unbothered nature of untroubled sleep. A single look at his placid face and he decided he'd never tell him his maternal grandmother was in a humid, Floridian women's prison.

He decided to write a quick response:

Hello,

You don't know me, but I was living with your daughter, Jeanette.

She no longer lives at this address. If you do hear from her, please tell her...

He stopped. Tell her what?

...please tell her, I hope she's well.

He knew Adele would want him to rage, to tell her about Albert, to exact painful revenge. He simply wanted to let her know he hadn't forgotten. He signed his name and slipped it into the apartment's mailbox the following morning.

◇

Marian came and stayed with him for a weekend.

"How are you?" she asked, balancing Albert on her knee. He was almost two now, fully mobile and active.

"I'm doing okay. I've finally struck a balance with my class schedule, the nanny, mum being completely overbearing."

"You look skinny."

"I'm busy, but I also started running. Once in the morning and once when I get home from work."

"Well, that explains it. A replacement for something else? Or someone else?"

Oliver didn't respond.

"Well, are you still seeing her?"

Sofi. Oliver had unfairly blamed her for a time, refusing her phone calls. Eventually, she intuited what had transpired through mutual friends and turned up at his doorstep with a bottle of wine. Neither of them asked questions and, instead, settled back into their routine fairly readily.

"I am."

"Alright. Well, I guess I can't blame you now, but it was really bad form Ollie. Jeanette was this fragile thing that you let Adele walk all over and then you dismissed her, I know, I know, but I'm not taking her side. I just want to warn you off repeating the whole fiasco over again."

"I'm trying not to," he assured her. "Sofi is focused on school, she doesn't want to be a mum right now. We see each other when it's convenient. She's sweet to Albie when she's here, we work on the magazine. And, by the way, I don't think Jeanette was ever all that fragile, not really."

"You might be right about that," she conceded with a shrug.

Marian bounced Albert on her knees again. He started burbling and squirming to be let down, then ran full force into the edge of the sofa, falling backward on his soft head. There was a long pause while he gathered the necessary strength, then a forceful wail shook the interior of Oliver's apartment.

"He's got a set of pipes," Marian commented.

Oliver scooped him up, assessed the nonexistent damage, then, once the squall ceased, he released him to toddle around with his blocks.

Marian had escaped to the kitchen to avoid the screaming.

"Hey, who's this letter from? Do you have a prison pen pal?"

"What?"

She held a stack of mail the housekeeper had collected for him, on top was a letter from the same women's prison as before. An electric charge of recognition ran up his spine. He subdued it.

"Oh, that. No, I just make a donation."

"Mr. Generosity," Marian joked.

The moment she left, Oliver tore into the envelope. Inside was another neatly folded letter on the same thick paper with the same looping cursive in fine point Sharpie pen.

Hello Oliver,

I know who you are. She told me about you. I'm sorry to hear things didn't work out.

Here's a photo, I got two copies so I could send ya one.

Stay Well.

He shook the envelope upside down and a newspaper article, neatly clipped and folded into quarters, fell out.

The Walstrom Gallery welcomes Jeanette Victoria at her fi st solo show.

Jeanette's paintings welcome the darker side of the female psyche and embrace the juxtaposition of death and mundanity that transpires in everyday life.

The rest of the article had been cut off, though it was clearly a short write up. Just above, there was a black and white picture of Jeanette, unmistakably her, in a form-fitting black dress, her hair straight and neat. She was flanked by the gallery owners and smiled shyly at the camera.

A volley of emotions loosed itself inside of him: rage, envy, adoration, all of the things that would send one straight to Dante's hell.

He placed the note, the picture, in the drawer with Jeanette's original post-it note and tried not to think of it again.

Oliver proposed to Sofi two days after she graduated.

Adele had given him both the ring and her blessing. Marian had finally met her and decided she wasn't all that bad. Albert called her Sofsti and happily let her play with his favorite toys.

They had flutes of champagne with her folks who were still in town for the graduation and Oliver found himself wishing, only for a moment, that they could have shared a cheap beer, alone, in the corner of some dingy bar. Those days, he accepted, were over.

He loved Sofi for being something other than that though. She was classy and polished and well-read and kind. She told him she loved Albert and couldn't wait to give him a little sister.

"We're going to be so happy," she assured him. "And I think we should take Albie to the park tomorrow, to celebrate."

"That would be really nice," Oliver agreed, kissing her on the lips.

She left with her parents, who were staying at a hotel and not privy to the fact that Sofi already mostly lived at his apartment.

Once everyone had gone, he began to walk. He walked through the park, past other couples touching hands, arms, lips. He walked past the area known for after hours drug deals, past the burger place he used to go to near campus. He walked until he found himself outside Jeanette's old apartment. A broken down car sat on blocks in the parking lot, maybe being worked on by its' owner, maybe a victim of tire theft, he couldn't tell. Tin foil covered many of the windows in an attempt to blot out sunlight, or reality.

He closed his eyes and saw the morning sun shining through the metal bars on her back window, the window sill where she grew her plants, a prison she'd created for herself and didn't want to leave. Originally, he'd immediately deemed the place utterly depressing, but she brought so much cheer and personality to it, nothing else mattered after a while.

He walked on, past the apartment, to the corner store she frequented for cigarettes, saltines, booze, ice pops in the summer. He decided to buy a soda, drink it on his way home.

Behind the counter an older Indian man sat watching television, effectively ignoring Oliver who stood with a glass bottle Coke sweating in his hand. He felt certain Jeanette had mentioned this guy before, did his name start with an R, or a V? Oliver almost cleared his throat in frustrated protest, but instead his eyes drifted past the man's head to a painting hanging over the cash register. Dark and layered, he immediately recognized it as one of the small object paintings from Jeanette's show. A show he'd skipped out of spite to be with Sofi.

"One dollar," the man said.

"What?"

"One dollar, please."

"Oh, right." Oliver handed him the money, his hands shaking as though he'd seen a ghost.

He felt the man's eyes on his back as he disappeared back out onto the sidewalk. The Coke burned the back of his throat, his mouth felt sweaty and he sucked in the air to try and quell his inner disquiet.

Once Sofi officially moved in, a few weeks before the wedding, she undertook the task of deep cleaning their living space. At first, Oliver suspected she was engaging in the age-old art of nesting, and that was part of it, but it was also a purging, a taking stock.

On the second day of this madness, Oliver saw the orange lipstick tipped cigarette in the kitchen trash, artfully placed on top, daring him to comment. He simply closed the garbage lid and went back to his office.

On the third day, he saw the writeup online.

"Jeanette Victoria's revelatory solo show to take place at the Opal Gallery in downtown LA, Friday 7pm."

He slammed the laptop, trapping the past inside it.

Then, he reopened it and booked a roundtrip train ticket for that Friday.

He told Sofi he was going to visit Marian and Thomas for a final single-cousins get-together. Sofi approved. She asked if she could invite some of her own friends over for a little get together as well. He didn't mind at all.

Oliver stood on the train platform in the crisp morning with an air of guilt about him. He'd spent quite a lot of his recent romantic life feeling guilty in one way or another, and this time it felt particularly silly. He wasn't going to try and sleep with Jeanette, it was clear she didn't want him, but he needed to see her. And this was a feeling he could not explain to Sofi, the woman who had thrown out her cigarettes just two days prior. He had the late night train booked back and did not intend to deviate from his plan. Just a glimpse, to make sure she'd been real.

The Opal Gallery was one of glitz and glamour, huge chandeliers hung from the ceiling and lights of appropriately opalescent colors left their trails on the wall before switching directions and swirling off opposite him again. People thronged the gallery space, there were three rooms, all open for viewing, and Jeanette's was the only one without white walls. They'd painted everything eggplant, dark purple and black, and her paintings, all of them, hung in groups. Some of the bigger ones, majestically, hung alone.

Oliver recognized much of her earlier work, but the recent studies were mostly nude women laid across that same red afghan she'd used in the earlier dead flower still life paintings. Still, a floral motif pervaded much of her work, the close relationship of lust and mundanity, eroticism and ordinariness, death and darkness and life together. He tried to view each piece objectively, trying not to seek himself in it, somewhere. Nothing male survived in this new world Jeanette envisioned and he tried not to take it personally.

She slunk in quietly, standing against the wall. Still, he sensed her presence. He watched as she spoke to the gallery owner, shook someone's hand, laughed. He couldn't hear her, but the sound of her laugh echoed in his head like a bell of memory. She wore all black, of course, a simple shift dress, spiked heels, and her customary lipstick seemed darker than usual. She was always one to try and capture a mood, Oliver acknowledged.

Suddenly, her head lifted, like a gazelle smelling a predator. She looked one way, then the other, and finally directly at him, standing like a fool in the center of the room, clutching a glass of wine.

Her eyes widened, but she didn't smile or shout, her mouth etched itself into a perfectly arched smirk. She raised a glass to him and inclined her head in salute. He raised his class back. The gallery owner stepped into their line of vision and began speaking to her again.

Oliver wove his way through the crowd, back outside, and into the night.

Sofi and Oliver edited four editions of *Parabolas* together, each one gaining more traction than the last. Sofi managed their advertisement.

"Nothing too garish, we need a bit of pretension," she assured him.

The submissions just kept rolling in.

After some gentle coaxing, Travis came back and reprised his role as co-editor. Sofi made sure to make him feel extra included and Oliver didn't insist on publishing his own work anymore.

When Sofi became pregnant, she desperately wanted to

redecorate everything and fussily complained to Oliver about the "outdatedness" of their website.

"It's fine."

"It's worse than the apartment."

Which she had hired someone to completely repaint two weeks prior while she stayed at Adele's to avoid the fumes. Adele, who normally would have balked at an intruder, made Sofi smoothies and watched daytime television with her. They played with Albert, who was starting Montessori pre-school soon, at Adele's demand, and took him to the park in the afternoon. Oliver was left to deal with the workers and slept with his window open to avoid a headache.

He did have to admit, the apartment looked more modern, and *Parabolas* could use a facelift.

"You'll have to sort the archive and save everything first," Travis told him. "I don't need you yelling at me because I lost one of your love notes in the redesign."

"Fine."

Oliver stayed up late for a couple of nights backing up their archives.

He remembered perfectly each piece they'd published and creating a desktop folder of past work, retaining their meticulous formatting, made him proud. *Parabolas* was his third child, or really his first.

He paused at the issue that he and Sofi had both contributed to. It seemed like such a very long time ago they'd published these pieces, and they were soppy. Oliver considered deleting them, keeping them private, ultimately deciding it wouldn't be entirely in line with his own morals as editor.

Then, he noticed an abnormality — a poem he hadn't published.

"Rotten Hearts" was the title.

He panicked, had someone hacked the site? Truthfully, he had to admit he'd been using the same password, on the same server for years, so anyone with access to his laptop could easily have accessed it. A joke from Travis, surely.

He moused over the title. Clicked.

"Rotten Hearts"

We all know
    the archetype of the drowned woman.

But who knows
of the pain it takes to become her?

La Llorona:
    desperately weeping, calls children to her arms,
    only because she so desperately misses her own.

Ophelia:
who drowns herself, perhaps by accident, perhaps not,
    her body suspended by the tenuous willow branch.

Edna Pontellier:
    who walks out into the ocean alone,
     leaving her husband and children on the beach behind her.

Then, there are all the women
    who have drowned standing up,
    breathing only air.

They stand where I stood,
     lungs filling wi h gasps of pure oxygen,
    still unable to breathe, to live, to thrive.

They died a little at a time,

    inside, where no one could see.

About the Author

Abigail Stewart is a fiction writer from Berkeley, California. She lives with her partner in an apartment filled with plants and books and breakable things. *The Drowned Woman* is her debut novel.

About the Publisher

Whisk(e)y Tit is committed to restoring degradation and degeneracy to the literary arts. We work with
authors who are unwilling to sacrifice intellectual rigor, unrelenting playfulness, and visual beauty in our
literary pursuits, often leading to texts that would otherwise be abandoned in today's largely homogenized
literary landscape. In a world governed by idiocy, our commitment to these principles is an act of civil service
and civil disobedience alike.